ONE OF LIFE'S JOURNEYS

BY WELDON JAMES

Published by Starry Night Publishing.Com

Rochester, New York

Copyright 2019 Weldon James

This book remains the copyrighted property of the author, and may not be reproduced, copied and distributed for commercial, or noncommercial purposes. Thank you for your support.

Weldon James

Also by Weldon James

The Incident at Pine Lake

This book is dedicated to my beloved Donna who patiently supported this endeavor. Thanks Honey!

Weldon James

Weldon James

the school played other schools in their league, they would be on the same bus together. They enjoyed each other's company and looked forward to the time that they spent together representing Manchester Memorial High.

Graduation from Manchester Memorial High School was a day to celebrate. Beside the traditional pomp and circumstance, it ushered a new group of young people into the local work force, which was certainly good for the Manchester economic outlook. On this very special day in June of 1968 both John Young and Cathy Greco were about to leave the trappings of academic life and assume their roles in the real world. John would be looking to join his Dad at the Manchester Locomotive Company while Cathy had applied for a job with the Granite State Federal Credit Union. Two days before graduation, she had received her notice that she had been hired starting July first.

The Greco family, in recognition of their daughter's graduation, planned a party out at the Lake for their friends and family. Cathy was also allowed to invite her friends and she did. Fellow tracker John Young was included with his parents. About sixty people were there to share in the festivities of the day. The weather, as usual, provided a lovely day to celebrate and party at the Lake.

Weldon James

CHAPTER 2

Joe Greco and Bob Young had become friends, thanks to their children, John and Cathy knowing each other. The Young family was often invited to "cookouts" at the Lake. After one such cookout in early August, Bob was invited to join Joe on a trip to Boston for the annual boat show. Joe and Lucy Greco had decided to get a pontoon boat to tour the Lake. With the season coming to an end, there was no better time than now to pursue the issue.

"Since the season is almost over, maybe we will be lucky and find some boats on sale," said Joe.

"Looks like our kids get along pretty good," commented Bob Young.

"Yeah, they seem to enjoy each other's company," said Joe Greco. "By the way Bob, how does it feel working with your Son?"

"Great," said Bob. "Not because I'm his Father, but he is very quick on the pickup and is learning to do the job with ease and accuracy," he added. "I assume that Cathy is doing well at the Credit Union downtown."

Joe countered with, "She seems to be adapting to the regimen without a problem. It's another learning experience for her and I'm sure she'll do well." Additional chatter filled the time spent as they headed toward Boston.

As they toured the convention display rooms, it became apparent to Bob that Joe was going to buy a boat today. He finally settled on a twenty four foot Crest built pontoon boat, which sported a Johnson seventy five horsepower outboard engine. After negotiating a price and a delivery date, Joe and Bob left the convention center for the ride home.

At the first available service station Joe decided to gas up for the ensuing trip. He also bought a six pack of "Pabst's Blue Ribbon" beer for the trip. The men shared their stories and their beer as they proceeded toward Derry and Bob's house. The trip had become quite a bonding session for both.

The remainder of that boating season was short lived. Winter was about to rear its ugly head if you were a boater. But it was welcomed by those who enjoy all the events that come with snow and the cold. In this case, Cathy and John enjoyed both seasons. John had saved his money and had gotten an older 1959 Ford coupe for travelling to and from work, home and Cathy's house. They had become very close and were now dating only each other. Both sets of parents were aware of the friendship and were happy with the choices that their kids seem to be making.

Later that week, John thought it appropriate to talk with Cathy about an issue he had been concerned about for a while. What with the war going on in Vietnam, he was sure that he would receive a draft notice very soon. That evening he and Cathy had a long talk about the war and what his options might be. Would he be better to wait to be drafted and be sent anywhere the government thought they needed him, or should he sign up with a specific branch of the service that he thought he could embrace? This was the first time they had had a discussion as serious as this. They both decided to reflect on the conversation and the possible implications involved and discuss it tomorrow night when they met to go dancing.

The next night, being a Saturday, meant that there was a dance up in Hookset at the local American Legion Hall. It usually drew about eighty people who, after several visits began to recognize each other as fellow dance fans. Cathy was quiet as they left her house and headed north. John, who hadn't had a lot of sleep the night before, was wondering what was going through Cathy's mind and how she felt about last night's discussion.

"How are you doing tonight, hon?" asked John.

"I didn't sleep all that well last night," she replied.

"Me either," said John.

The only thing they heard for the next ten miles was the purring of the motor. Obviously, they were both upset with the subject that was brought up and discussed last night and were still reflecting on it. Usually they were both chattering away when driving somewhere.

"Let's not spoil the evening. I still have some time to explore it more thoroughly before making a decision," said John. "Let's just have a good time tonight and dance our brains out," he quipped.

Cathy feigned a smile and nodded her head as they drove into the Legion parking lot.

Both Cathy and Bob seemed to be somewhat tired after last night, so they decided to leave before the dance was over. On the way back to Cathy's house they stopped at Morrison's Pharmacy to get a banana split. The store didn't close until midnight on Friday and Saturday nights and usually was filled with other young people out for an evening enjoying themselves.

After entering, they saw Terry Sloan and Jim Richards, also graduates, who invited them to sit with them. John immediately took advantage of the invite and sat down next to Jim. Cathy, recognizing the move by John, said "hello," and sat next to Terry. The conversation was about their new jobs and how all of them were doing. John bragged to Jim and Terry about his "new" car and how great it was to have one. The chatter lasted for about an hour when John said they were going to leave. He had to go to work tomorrow, even though it was Sunday, and needed to get some sleep. Getting some overtime really helped with the finances and the special little item that John was saving up for.

Terry and Jim were fellow graduates from the Manchester Memorial High School and had both gotten jobs at the Anderson Buick dealership in Manchester. They had been recognized as a couple for several years when in school. Jim was a football player and Terry had earned a varsity letter from her display of gymnastics while on the cheerleading team. Both couples had become friends and were spotted at many venues together.

John and Cathy realized that they really loved each other as evidenced by the fact that they wanted to spend all their free time together. Time seemed to fly, as it always does, when you are involved in an emotional relationship.

John had become a valuable employee at the Manchester Locomotive Company, constantly being offered more challenging jobs to accomplish. His Dad was very proud of him.

Cathy had learned a lot about the workings of a Credit Union. It didn't take her long to draw the parallel between her job and a job at any bank. She was very quickly adjusting to her job and her new responsibilities.

Winter had arrived early this year in New Hampshire. The mornings reflected the big drop in temperatures and the Lake was starting to show a little ice around the shallow shorelines. Right after Thanksgiving, both the Greco and Young families started to get ready for the coming Christmas holidays. Joe Greco had already taken the pontoon boat out of the water and had it covered with a huge tarp. It was up on old tires that were being used as a dry dock for the winter. With the engine winterized and in the shed, he was ready for next year.

Lucy Greco kept busy decorating their home, while she made batch after batch of various styles of Christmas cookies.

One of Life's Journeys

Doris and Bob Young were equally engaged in getting ready for the holidays. Their daughters, Amy and Paula, would make it home for a visit. Everyone was looking forward to the wonderful times the whole family experienced during these visits.

Weldon James

CHAPTER 3

The Christmas holidays, with all their pomp and circumstance, passed quickly. The families celebrated both separately and together, as they had become good friends. John and Cathy shared meaningful gifts that were not very expensive. After all, they had just started working about six months ago and were into the savings mode. Being able to buy new clothes seemed to be a luxury and the dominant item.

A group of high school graduates decided to spend New Year's Eve together. A party was quickly organized and those who participated had a great time. Everyone who had attended got home OK and the night was considered a success.

The last week in January, Joe and Lucy Greco left for their annual two week vacation in Florida. Cathy remained at home out at the Lake. She was not afraid since she and John would be seeing each other even more often.

During those two weeks John and Cathy talked all about their relationship, where they hoped it would go, the possibility of it becoming a permanent one and about their collective future as a family and even how many kids they would like to have. It was during those two weeks that they became lovers and reflected many times on that experience. It had been the first time for both.

Joe and Lucy returned to New Hampshire on February thirteenth, the day before St. Valentine's Day. Coincident with their return, the Youngs had received a crate of Florida grapefruit that had been sent by Lucy and Joe. During the thank you phone call, the Youngs heard all about the trip to

Florida and they were asked to consider going with them next year. It certainly sounded like a fun trip and a way to get away from all the snow and cold weather for a little while.

February fourteenth, 1969, began as a dark, gloomy winter day in Manchester. It was good that it was a Saturday which meant no one had to get up early and travel to work. John had invited Cathy to go out that night. She asked where they were going, and the reply was that it was a surprise. It hadn't snowed in a couple of days, so the roads were in good shape. This meant that the reservation that had been made by John was going to be filled. As they approached town, John asked Cathy not to peek until they had arrived at the location. He pulled over in front of an old, but very good restaurant, known as the Hanover Street Chophouse.

Cathy finally opened her eyes and saw the restaurant marquee and commented that neither she nor her family had ever been there but that they had heard good reports about the food and the service. She couldn't wait to exit the car and get inside where it was warmer.

The maître d' led the couple to a table in front of the huge fireplace that was glowing brightly in the darkened dining area. How romantic, thought Cathy.

A neatly dressed waiter approached the table, welcomed them to the restaurant and asked if they wanted anything to drink before ordering. John was quick to answer that they would have something with their dinner and they just needed to take a few minutes to scan the menu. The waiter passed a menu to Cathy first and then one to John. He said he would return shortly.

Cathy was the first to talk. She said, "This is a beautiful place. Thank you for bringing me here."

"Yeah, it is a nice place and the food is great," commented John. As they scanned the menu, they could feel the heat coming from the fireplace.

"What are you going to have John?" queried Cathy.

"I'm thinking about a nice steak. I've had one here before and it was perfect. It comes with a small salad and a baked potato," said John. "Cathy, please have anything you see that strikes your fancy," continued John. "Tonight, is our night to celebrate honey."

Cathy wondered what he meant by that statement. We celebrate each time we are together.

They both ordered a steak dinner that was delicious. The house salad was crisp and fresh and the baked potato with sour cream was fine. After the main meal, both ordered a dish of raspberry ice cream topped with just a hint of chocolate sauce. What a lovely ending to a lovely meal.

While they were still relaxing in front of the fireplace and the warmth it generated, John leaned forward and started a conversation that ultimately brought tears to Cathy's eyes. He said, "Cathy, we've known each other for several years now and I want you to know how much I love you and how much happiness you've brought into my life. Without you, life would just be a drag. I want to marry you and raise a family with only you. Will you be my wife?"

With that said, he pulled a small box from his jacket, opened it up and presented a beautiful diamond engagement ring to the woman he wanted for his wife. He leaned forward and kissed Cathy softly on the lips. He heard a stifled murmur as tears started to flow.

Cathy sat back and said, "Yes, John. I will be proud to be your wife." With that said, they both shared a quiet moment thinking about what had just happened.

The ride back to Lake Massabesic was slowly deliberate on John's part so that they could enjoy their time together. The heater in the car was keeping the cold air from ruining the mood while the radio was playing some very relaxing soft music. Cathy snuggled next to John in the front seat. They were very happy as they talked about the future together and their plans. John pulled up to the brightly lit home at the Lake. He leaned over and kissed Cathy good night and said he would see her tomorrow. She exited the Ford and ran into the house. After all, she had something to show her Mom and Dad. John backed down the gravel driveway and headed home. This will be a Saturday I'll never forget, thought John.

On Sunday morning, John shared with his parents what had happened last night at the restaurant and Cathy's response. Both Bob and Doris were somewhat surprised but very happy for John. They remarked about how lovely and nice Cathy was.

Doris said, "I can't wait to tell Amy and Paula about this. Your sisters will be so happy for you."

Bob shook his son's hand and said that if there was anything he needed, that he was there for him. The parents soon learned that no date had been discussed for the wedding. John knew that he still had to make a decision that could affect any plans from materializing soon. He and Cathy still had some business to resolve before selecting a date.

After taking a shower and getting cleaned up, John and his family got into the family car for the ride to St. Raphael's Catholic Church in Manchester. It was Sunday morning and they were headed for the eleven o'clock Mass. To their surprise, they spotted the Greco family in the third pew. Both families received communion. After church, they stopped in the warm vestibule to say hello. Handshakes and congratulations were abundant. While the women and Bob were talking, John motioned to Cathy's Father to come closer. When Joe arrived next to John, they turned and walked back into the church.

When they stopped, John extended his hand and said, "Mr. Greco, I apologize for not asking for Cathy's hand in marriage before last night. I do want to marry Cathy and she wants to become my wife. I hope I have your blessing."

Joe responded with, "John, you have my blessing and I know you and Cathy will be a happy, loving couple. You will be the son Lucy and I never had. Thank you for who you are and I look forward to the big day."

Weldon James

CHAPTER 4

The remainder of the winter and early spring was dedicated to the preparations for the wedding which was finally scheduled for Saturday, September twenty ninth, 1969, at St. Raphael's Catholic Church in Manchester. Many weekends were spent deciding who would be invited and where those from out of town would stay.

The Grecos, with the full backing of the Young family, decided they would like to host the reception on their property out at the Lake. This meant renting a huge tent with a portable dance floor that could easily serve the purpose. Time was spent talking with caterers since Joe had put his foot down on any involvement by Lucy. He wanted her to enjoy the day and not have to worry about cooking or serving anybody.

A commitment by a locally recognized band was negotiated and hours were spent determining the flowers that would be needed.

Both John and Cathy decided to limit the wedding party to just six people. Cathy had asked Terry Sloan to be her maid of honor and Amy and Paula, John's sisters, to be bridesmaids in the wedding party. Likewise, John had asked Jim Richards to be the best man. The ushers' jobs went to fellow employees George Williams and Curt Brown, both of whom work with John at the Locomotive Company. John, Curt and George had become friends during the past year. They all worked together in the same division. One of Joe Greco's brothers volunteered to be the bartender. Even the glassware was going to be rented from the catering company.

Throughout the spring and into the summer, both John and Cathy were inseparable. They did everything together and were obviously so much in love. They had spent time talking about their honeymoon and where they would like to go. Locations ranged from Cape Cod to Mount Washington in upper New Hampshire. They also ranged from New York City to Niagara Falls in New York State. They finally settled on a grand old hotel in Osterville, Massachusetts, which is out on Cape Cod. It would be out of season, since most people who frequented the Cape had to return to the mainland to prepare for school or go back to work. This meant that the Cape would be available for them to explore as much as they cared to. They even thought of taking the ferry out of Hyannis to Martha's Vineyard on one of their side trips. All in all, the past six months had become very exciting.

One of the last things for Cathy to consider was the wedding gown she would be wearing on the day she got married. She and her Mom finally decided to go to Boston and visit several bridal shops. On their second trip they hit pay dirt and came home with the dress. Gowns were selected for the maid of honor and the bridesmaids. One last thing to consider was the fitting of those dresses to their owners. A trip to achieve that goal had been negotiated.

Now, the only thing to be concerned about was the weather. No matter what the weather, the Grecos were relieved that the planning was just about over, commitments made, and they could look forward to the "big" day.

During the past several months, enlisting in the service that John was considering doing, was discussed quite thoroughly. He and Cathy came to the conclusion that he should remain at home, not enlist and wait to be called, if in fact he was going to be. Being a married person had changed the equation and the responsibilities commensurate with the commitment were enough for him to withdraw from further consideration. He would soon be a married guy and being a newlywed should be his priority.

Time had been spent in searching for a place the Youngs would call home. They had been very fortunate in finding a vacant, two bedroom apartment in downtown Manchester. This was close to work for both and would serve as home until they could afford to buy a small starter home somewhere in the suburbs.

Weldon James

CHAPTER 5

A crowd had gathered outside of St Raphael's Roman Catholic Church on Walker Street in Manchester, New Hampshire. Today the Greco family and the Young family were there to witness the joining of the families. The weather was bright and lovely on this sunny day in late September. George Williams and Curt Brown were already helping people down the aisles to their pews. They were dressed in white jacketed tuxedos and looked very sharp.

John and his best man, Jim, arrived and entered the church through the sacristy entrance. Father Moran was just dressing for the service. He said, "How are you doing today, John?"

John responded by saying he was a little nervous but finally happy to be there.

Organ music was heard as the church started to fill with those attending the wedding. Both John's Mom and Dad and Cathy's Mom were escorted to their pews. George and Curt had done a great job in escorting people to their seats. It was now time for them to remain in the back of the church and await the rest of the wedding party.

Within two or three minutes a black Cadillac arrived in front of the church with the rest of the wedding party. Cathy and her Dad exited the limo and started to climb the three steps that led to the foyer of the church. At last, the time had come for her to start to share her life with John.

Father Moran and two altar boys entered the altar area from the sacristy. When observed by the organist, the bridal march music started. George and Curt with Amy and Paula led the procession down the aisle followed by Terry Sloan, the maid of honor.

Joseph Greco took his daughter's arm and escorted her down the aisle. People attending the ceremony stood and faced the bride and her Dad as they passed. There was a faint murmur of approval at what they observed. Cathy looked absolutely stunning.

The groom and his best man had already entered the church and were positioned at the opening to the altar. When the Grecos reached the altar, Cathy's Dad lifted her veil and kissed her. He then passed her hand to John. John and Cathy approached the altar, inside the rail, while Joe stepped to his place next to his wife Lucy, who was in the first pew.

Father Moran approached the bride and groom and the civil portion of the wedding began. Upon completion of the exchanging of the vows, Father Moran started a Mass that symbolized the marriage in the eyes of God. The ceremony concluded when the Mass was over, and the organist finished her rendition of Ave Maria. The bride and groom started down the aisle, arm in arm, to the applause of those in attendance. When outside, they went down to the sidewalk area and started to receive the congratulations and well wishes of the people who exited the church.

Mr. and Mrs. John Young left in the limo to have pictures taken at a local photographer while the Grecos and Youngs proceeded out to the Lake and the reception that followed. All in all, it has been a beautiful wedding. The weather was perfect, and everyone was looking forward to relaxing and partying.

The bride and groom arrived about forty-five minutes after the reception had started. Joe's brother, the bartender, started to pop the champagne. When everyone had a glass, the best man gave a toast. The caterer provided a wonderful spread of delicious foods while the music played and people danced. Shortly thereafter, Cathy assembled those young ladies who would be of marrying age, turned her back to them, and tossed her bouquet. It was caught by her new sister-in-law, Paula Young. The party continued into the evening hours.

The Youngs left for their honeymoon about six thirty. They were on their way to Cape Cod. The first night would be spent in Boston at the Lennox Hotel, then on to the Cape.

Weldon James

CHAPTER 6

The Youngs finally checked into their room at the Lennox Hotel. The day had become very tiring and it didn't take them long to decide to have a final wedding drink and get to bed. After a remarkable evening of love making by both, they fell fast asleep.

The phone in their room rang at precisely eight o'clock the next morning. Without the wakeup call they would have slept all morning. They had travel plans which precluded sleeping half the day away. Taking showers and dressing took all of fifteen minutes and they were on their way to breakfast and their trip to the Cape.

An hour later they crossed the Bourne Bridge and onto Cape Cod. Reservations had been made at a lovely old hotel in Osterville, just outside of Hyannisport. The room was very comfortable and a great "home base" to explore the rest of the Cape from. Their plans included driving to Provincetown out at the tip of the Cape as well as a ferry boat ride to Martha's Vineyard. This was not only going to be their honeymoon but was going to count as their vacation.

The food at the hotel was very tasty and the rooms were clean and in great shape. All in all, they had a wonderful time. They both remarked about how quickly the week had gone. They had gotten a few inexpensive trinkets while out at Martha's Vineyard. These would be distributed to family members on both sides.

It didn't take long for their trip back home and the return to the life of reality. The apartment at 150 Green Spring Lane in Manchester had been somewhat furnished by both families before the wedding. The only new item was the bedroom set that John and Cathy bought. The rest of the furniture was a compilation of good condition hand-me-downs from the parents. The pressing thing to do now was to hang some curtains for their privacy. Cathy vowed she would accomplish that job tomorrow.

Monday morning at both work locations was filled with questions from their fellow employees and answers from John and Cathy. After sharing their honeymoon adventures, it didn't take very long for the newlyweds to get back into their work routines. One of the first thoughts Cathy had was, what am I going to cook for dinner tonight. She figured a great starter would be a meatloaf. There was no way she could screw that up. It was nothing more than a great big hamburger cooked in a small baking pan. The first meal went off without a hitch and was thoroughly enjoyed by the new Mr. & Mrs. Young.

Fall was quickly evolving into winter as the days were getting shorter and the evenings cooler. Work was now a routine for both the Youngs and they were doing very nicely at their respective jobs.

The U.S. mail that was delivered on Saturday, the last week of November however, changed many things for the newlyweds. John received his draft notice and was being called to active duty. He was instructed to report to the induction office in Manchester to be sworn in on Monday, the fifteenth of December.

That weekend will always be remembered by both the Youngs and the Grecos as the weekend from hell. So many questions needed to be answered for both families. Do I go into the Army or do I have a choice of the branch of service that I want to serve in? What happens to my job while I am away? Will it be there when I return? How long do I have to stay in the service? What happens to my wife?

The list of questions was endless. It was obvious that Cathy would probably move back with her Mom and Dad while John was away. They all thought that it was the intelligent thing to do. It certainly would give John and Cathy the opportunity to save some more money since she wouldn't have to pay any rent.

The next two weeks were filled with so much investigating and planning for the Youngs that before they knew it, they were spending the last weekend that they would spend together for a long time to come. Friday after work, the guys that John worked with gave him a small going away party. He was home with Cathy by ten o'clock. On Saturday evening the Greco and Young families came together to share a farewell dinner with Cathy and John. Sunday would be the day for just the two of them. They still had so many things left to share before time ran out.

While with the families on Saturday evening, Cathy and John decided to share a secret that they had just learned. Cathy was pregnant with their first child. She was due on the fourteenth of July, next year. The reactions and feelings of everyone present were so mixed. This was wonderfully happy news that they all reacted to. At the same time, it became even more of a concern since John was going to be inducted into the service in two days. That coupled with the fact that he may not be home for their first Christmas together as a family also dampened the wonderful news of Cathy's pregnancy. However, they all responded with the normal congratulations and kept the service issue out of the conversation. Both the Grecos and the Youngs remarked about the fact that they were going to be grandparents for the first time. The visit ended on a high note as John and Cathy left for their last night together for a long time to come.

Weldon James

PART TWO

SERVING OUR COUNTRY

Weldon James

CHAPTER 1

John was dropped off at the Manchester, New Hampshire draft board offices on Canal Street in downtown Manchester at about eight forty five on Monday morning. There were several other inductees also in the waiting room area. At precisely nine o'clock, a person wearing a uniform emerged from an adjoining office and started to call out names. After responding to the roll call, the inductees were told to line up and follow the recruiter into an office down the hallway. There they were checked by an Army Doctor for their condition and whether they would be accepted for service. Once finished with that chore, the draftees were returned to the main room. Two were not fit for service and were separated from the group. The remaining draftees were told to raise their right hand and repeat the swearing in oath. Once completed, the group was told that now they belonged to the U.S. Army and would be leaving for the First Army Training Center that was located at Fort Dix, New Jersey. Their bus would be leaving within twenty minutes.

John grabbed a seat on the bus next to a Roger Templeton who happened to be from Pembroke, New Hampshire. They engaged in conversation as the bus wound its way down thru Massachusetts, Connecticut, New York and finally into New Jersey. It was about four thirty in the afternoon when they arrived. They were deposited in front of a series of older wooden, two story buildings that looked like they may have been left over from World War II. There were a few more uniformed men, who John assumed were soldiers, waiting outside of the bus. They were asked for their names as they exited the bus. The entire group of inductees very quickly learned that these soldiers were Cadre and would be their trainers, and that they would have complete control of their every waking moment.

John and Roger were assigned to the second platoon of "C" Company, of the 880th Field Artillery Battalion, of the 364th Infantry Regiment, of the 69th Division Infantry Division. The 69th Infantry Division was responsible for the training of all the inductees from the entire First Army area which included all the Northeastern States. Sergeant Bowers would be their Drill Instructor.

It didn't take long before John and Roger, as well as the rest of the trainees, to understand that you did what you were told and when you were told. This was not a democratic environment and nothing that you were ordered to do was up for debate or discussion. Even though there were a lot of adjustments made, coupled with a lot of bitching, the men realized that what they had to go through was for their collective benefit and could make the difference between life and death, especially if they were assigned to a combat area.

Christmas came and went as did New Year's. The only contact available for the trainees was an occasional phone call home. John took as much advantage of that liberty as he could.

He finally received his first "pass" after six weeks of training. John and Roger got a ride to Trenton, New Jersey where they boarded a Pennsylvania Railroad train headed for Boston. Calls ahead alerted their families that they would be home for part of the weekend. Bob Young said he would meet them at the station. Roger could ride with the Youngs, as far as Manchester, where he would be picked up by his family. Both trainees knew that they had to be back at Fort Dix by reveille on Monday morning.

As they pulled into the Young's driveway in Derry, John spotted Cathy in the doorway of the home. He bolted from the car and ran to her. They embraced for what seemed to be several minutes before John introduced Roger. John's Dad offered to take Roger to Manchester for his pickup. Both men had determined that they needed to catch the four o'clock train out of Boston on Sunday to get back to Trenton on time. They said they would see each other at the station on Sunday.

Amy and Paula, John's sisters, had made it home for the visit by John. The only difference for them was that their "little" brother was wearing the uniform of a U.S. Army soldier.

After the usual family greetings coupled with the many questions about Ft. Dix and his training, John told the story of going through the infiltration course three times. The course, which simulates actual live firing of weapons and explosions was conducted once during the afternoon without the simulation. This dry run allowed the trainees to experience crawling on their backs under barbed wire with full equipment and carrying their rifle. The course was about fifty yards long. Later the "live" simulation occurred, once in daylight and once after dark. During these exercises, live 30 caliber ammunition was fired forty eight inches directly over the trainees' heads while quarter pound blocks of dynamite exploded all around them. The simulation is supposed to have the trainee experience what it could be like in an actual combat situation.

"It truly was a sobering experience for those who went through the course," said John. Those listening, readily agreed.

Doris Young had prepared a meal for them to take when they left to go to the Lake. John's visit happened to coincide with Cathy's parents' trip to Florida. This meant that they would have the privacy to come and go as they wanted and to do as they wanted. The next twenty four hours proved to be the best of times for both of them and it didn't start with a bugle playing reveille on Sunday morning.

As requested by his Dad, John and Cathy made it back to Derry by noon on Sunday. After kissing his Mother good bye,

John, Cathy and his Dad headed to the train station in Boston. It had been a great weekend. He was just sorry that it had to come to an end so soon. However, he did look forward to his next leave which would be in about in about two weeks after he finished basic training. He should get several days off before receiving his next set of orders.

CHAPTER 2

John and Roger got back to Fort Dix on time. Both men hit the "sack" and were asleep in no time. Cruel reveille disturbed the snoring at precisely six in the morning and the whole thing started all over again. March here, double time there and pay attention to what was being disseminated was the order of the day.

The next two weeks were filled with more of the same. One week was a bivouac session that lasted all week out on range road. John and Roger shared a pup tent since they were in the "field" all week. They experienced firing a variety of weapons which culminated by throwing live grenades onto a plowed field. The week passed very quickly for the trainees and before they realized it, they were back in their barracks. The last week of training was a combination of learning tactical issues and reinforcing what their responsibilities would be to the unit that they would ultimately be assigned to.

Written orders were received late on Friday evening of their last week in training. John's orders stated that he was to proceed from Fort Dix, New Jersey to Fort Benning, Georgia. His time of departure from Fort Dix was early Saturday morning with an arrival time at Fort Benning of no later than midnight on the following Wednesday. He and many of his fellow trainees were headed to Ft. Benning to continue their infantry training. Several trainees, however, were selected to proceed to other schools in many other locations in the U.S. Roger was one of those. He would proceed to Fort Sill,

Oklahoma for armor training. Provided with their new sets of orders, their basic training course at Fort Dix came to an end and they were on their way home for a couple of days before going to their next assignment.

One thing that John knew; he was going to miss the "hoagies" that they enjoyed on weekends from the little sandwich shop in Wrightstown which was located just outside of Fort Dix.

The trip home to New Hampshire was uneventful. John and Cathy spent just about all their free time together. They even had the opportunity to have a banana split at Morrison's Pharmacy. Cathy was feeling good and was really looking forward to becoming a Mom. John and she shared so many thoughts and ideas of things they would do when he was home and the war was over.

All too quickly, the visit back home went by and it was time for John to get on a plane in Boston and fly to Columbus, Georgia. John and Cathy left home at ten on Wednesday morning for Logan Airport in Boston. The couple was accompanied by Bob Young and Joe Greco. John's flight was scheduled for departure at two o'clock and was the only flight from Boston to Columbus that day. He had to be on time to make the flight. They arrived at the airport by noon and found a little restaurant just outside the waiting room area. After sharing a leisurely lunch, it was time to say the final good byes. Joe and Bob shook John's hand and wished him the best of luck. They requested that he keep in touch as often as he could.

John and Cathy embraced for several minutes. They reiterated their love for each other and there were tears in the eyes of both as they parted.

Cathy, her Dad and Bob walked slowly back to their car as John checked in and took a seat in the waiting room. His last "leave" for possibly a long time had come to an end. God, how he wished this whole damn thing would be over and he and Cathy could get on with their lives.

CHAPTER 3

The flight from Boston to Columbus was a little bumpy but the airline delivered its "cargo" on time. After retrieving his duffel bag, John made his way outside the terminal and hailed a cab. He was dropped off at the gate of Fort Benning and waited while the MP checked his orders. He was finally admitted and on his way to his new assignment area. His orders read that he had been assigned to the first platoon of George Company which was part of the second training Battalion.

He found the Company orderly room and proceeded to officially "check in". John would draw his equipment from the supply room and start to familiarize himself with his surroundings. He had been assigned to the third squad in the first platoon. This would be his home for at least the next eight weeks.

His training started the next morning with a wakeup call at five thirty. Oh my, here we go again thought John.

The training courses that John was going to be exposed to, were the standard training courses for getting soldiers ready for shipment to a conflict area and designated as replacement personnel. His training at this level included courses in hand to hand combat, survival training, demolition and heavy weapons training. Sgt. Jefferson, his Cadre training officer, was going to see that his people were going to be the best trained soldiers at Fort Benning. After all, he might just be reassigned from the training school at Benning and be assigned to stay with this group of soldiers as they headed toward Vietnam. Realizing that possibility, he was going to make sure that they were in top condition and well trained, particularly if they were going into combat with him.

The course ended after eight weeks of very intensive training and the group was ordered to proceed from Lawson Air Force base, which was located adjacent to Fort Benning, to Hamilton Air Force base in Novato, California. This was a major fly through base for troops slated to go to Vietnam. It was at this base that John was finally able to talk with Cathy for a longer time period. They had so much to say to each other. John was bought up to date as Cathy told him about all the goings-on in Manchester. They spent about twenty five minutes on the phone before John's time was up. Their good byes bought tears to both their eyes as they said goodnight and retired for the evening. They had promised to write each other every day, if they could. This was really all John had to look forward to as he departed for Saigon the next morning.

The newly trained soldiers arrived in Vietnam in the early hours of the morning on the twenty first of April. They were immediately assigned to a replacement company and taken to their bivouac area which was a grouping of squad sized tents just outside the airbase. From here they would be assigned as needed.

John and several of his fellow arrivals were immediately assigned to remain in the "repo" company before final assignment. Their function, until assigned to a line infantry unit, would be to assist in the logistics of supplying those Americans that were in the combat area. Day after day planes of the military air transport service would land in Saigon loaded with everything from food, clothing, ammunition and even Agent Orange, which was a defoliant used by the military to clear visual paths around manned "fire bases." The use of this chemical agent provided visibility of the surroundings and was one way of helping prevent surprise sneak attacks.

After about one month of unloading and loading plane after plane at the base, John's squad was given orders to proceed to Firebase Patton which was located just outside of a town called Cu Chi. The only "scuttlebutt" that John had heard was that Cu Chi was known as an area that was loaded with tunnels for access by the enemy. His new address was "A" company of the 2nd Battalion of the 14th Infantry Regiment of the 25th Infantry Division which was headquartered in Cu Chi. This town was located about 48 miles from Saigon and their mode of travel would be by helicopter since there were several "hot spots" between Saigon and Cu Chi if travelling by vehicle.

The squad collected their gear, had a last warm meal and was air lifted to Firebase Patton. Firebase Patton was located at a place referred to as "hobo woods" which was about 6 to 7 "clicks" outside the military headquarters in Cu Chi. As they approached the landing area, John could see that all the natural vegetation around the base had been cleared. This was done so no one could enter the area without being noticed. Once again, the new replacements were apprised of the fact that the entire area was heavily tunneled by the Viet Cong and that they must be alert all the time for infiltrators.

Hopefully this won't be too bad, he thought. He just wanted the time to go quickly so he could return home and be with Cathy and, the soon to be, new baby.

During the afternoon of his third day at this new base, the word came down that he and several others were going out on patrol that evening. The objective was to plant claymore mines on the access trails from the West being used by the enemy. He felt somewhat relieved that the other patrol members were not new to the area and were considered veterans. This would be a complete learning experience for him. His new squad leader was Sergeant Washington from Baltimore. He was regular Army and not a draftee. Sgt. Washington's next assignment was going to be attending the Officers Candidate

School back at Fort Benning. Upon completion, he would become a Second Lieutenant.

From time to time the squad would hear the crackle of small arms fire in the distance. They were headed in that direction. Booby trap training back at Fort Benning had really paid off. The squad was just about finished when a mortar shell, fired by the enemy, went off right in front of several squad members.

John felt a burning sensation in his left side just before he passed out. When he came to, he was being carried to a waiting Huey IV medical evacuation helicopter. His left side felt like it was burning, and he felt wet from the blood oozing from his wound. My God, what has happened to me, he thought. Once again, John passed out. The medic working on John checked his "dog tags" and determined that John was a type "O" blood recipient and started an intravenous transfusion. John had just about bled out. To say he was in critical condition would be an understatement.

The Huey landed at the "72nd" Field Hospital where John was immediately stabilized by the team of doctors in attendance. His wounds were so severe that he was quickly on his way to the larger evacuation hospital back in Saigon. After several days of close observation, it was decided that John needed to receive a complete workup by specialists and that would be done at the Camp Zana Army Hospital in Japan. His wounds were very serious and needed the attention of a series of different doctors. John, by this time, had regained a sense of what had happened to him and that the wounds would probably be, in the long run, very debilitating. God, what do I tell Cathy when I get home, he thought.

Once he was admitted to the hospital in Japan, teams of doctors and nurses visited him every day. He was being watched closely to see that he remained in a stable condition. All too often wounds of this magnitude claimed the victim's life. No one there was going to allow that to happen with this case.

After all the observations, it was determined that John would probably not be able to use his left arm ever again. His left side had been shattered by the blast and many, many pieces of shrapnel had torn his muscles and nerves almost to shreds. He would face many operations in the future and countless hours of rehab just to be able to resume an acceptable lifestyle.

During his stay in Japan, John communicated with his family on several occasions. They had been notified of his injuries by the Department of the Army. His first call was to Cathy. They discussed what had happened to John and what the future looked like for them once he was discharged.

While in the hospital in Japan, John learned that three members of his squad had been killed the night that they were placing the mines. One of those killed happened to be Sgt. Washington. God help these guys and their families, thought John. After a sobering reflection on the whole issue, he said to himself, "why?" He didn't come up with a logical answer.

Weldon James

CHAPTER 4

After what seemed to be a very long time, John was informed he was being sent to the Walter Reed Army Hospital in Bethesda, Maryland. Any procedures that were to be done to help repair his body would be administered there. John had become aware that it was going to take a long time to recover from this episode in his young life. Extended physical therapy and convalescing was also part of the picture for John. Will I ever be the same again, he wondered.

John finally arrived back in the Unites States and was taken directly to the Walter Reed facility in Bethesda, Maryland. He started the admission procedure which lasted about thirty minutes and was ultimately assigned to a "quad" room on the third floor in "K" wing of the Hospital. The "quad" room meant that he had three other men with him in the same room.

Cathy, together with the Greco and Young families, arrived at the Hospital about two hours after John's arrival. The timing was perfect because John had been processed and was in his room when they got there. To report that the initial meeting was an emotional one would be a gross understatement. Kisses and tears flowed like water. It was a moment in time that everyone would always remember.

Cathy leaned across the bed and gave John a loving kiss, telling him that she loved him and that everything would be all right. John said that he loved her and couldn't wait for the birth of their child since Cathy was really showing her pregnancy. She was so happy that John was home and that they would ultimately become a family with a child growing up in beautiful New Hampshire. God is good, she thought.

John, who was in a temporary body cast to immobilize his left side from any more damage, composed himself to assure those present that he was ultimately going to be OK. He talked about the procedures that he would have which would provide him with as much independence as they could in allowing him to resume a normal every day routine. He indicated that it would take some time to recoup from the injuries he received and that an extensive physical therapy agenda was part of the procedure. Cathy and the respective families listened to John and were relieved to hear his positive feelings about what would be happening and the expected resumption of a happy lifestyle.

After much conversation about what happened to him and all the help that was there for him, John started to yawn. The parents were the first to remark that they should leave to give John some time to rest. They decided that they would probably eat in the hospital cafeteria and return to visit after dinner. They had made reservations for the remainder of the week and were looking forward to spending as much time with John as was allowed.

Cathy and both set of parents left John and headed for the Hospital cafeteria. Their collective conversations while having their dinner were upbeat, as they tried to accept the life style changes that awaited everyone. They knew that John had major challenges ahead of him but that he was the kind of person who could cope with them and get on with his life. The fact that he was no longer in harm's way was a comforting thought for everyone. Thank God he's home. We can deal with all the rest.

The family stayed in Bethesda for the remainder of the week before returning to New Hampshire. They witnessed John's progress as he was being given physical therapy every day. They also saw a change in John's demeanor. He seemed to be at ease and a lot happier than when they arrived several days ago. What a good feeling they all were experiencing.

Soon it became time for those visiting John to say good bye and head for home. John was looking forward to returning to work in the Locomotive Company and being with his wife and child. Good byes were tearful but brief. John had his morning therapy session and they had a long trip to look forward to. No one had been able to answer one of the most important questions which was how long before John could leave and come home. There was still a lot of work to be done, so patience was the only answer.

It was a gloomy, rainy Thursday in Maryland several weeks later when the call came to John's room. Cathy was calling from the Manchester General Hospital to report that their daughter, Colleen Marie Young, weighing in at 7 pounds, 12 ounces had just been born. She reported that she and Colleen were doing just fine.

John was so moved by the report that he started to cry with extreme happiness. He had so wanted to be there for Cathy when the baby was born. However, that was not possible at this point. The Youngs and Grecos were with her when the baby was born. They all said hello to the new Dad and filled him in on his wonderful new daughter and their beautiful grandchild, Colleen.

Weldon James

CHAPTER 5

John had been operated on at least four times before his family made the trip south with Colleen. He had received many pictures over the last several months and couldn't wait to see his daughter and Cathy. They had spoken many times on the phone, as had his parents.

With any kind of luck, it would soon be time for him to come home to New Hampshire. He knew that he would initially be transferred to the Veteran's Hospital in Manchester. Once there, and with their help he hoped to resume a somewhat normal life again. He was made aware that he would probably never have use of his left arm again and would be in pain, from time to time, considering the major injuries that had shattered the left side of his body. Everything that was medically possible had been done to reestablish the use of his arm and hand, but to no avail. The only thing left was to get as much physical therapy as possible to strengthen his left arm.

Wonderful support groups are out there for permanently wounded servicemen and women. He would be contacting them as soon as possible. With their help and the help from everyone in his family, John was looking forward to regaining his place in the community. His primary concerns were about his wife Cathy and their daughter Colleen.

In early spring of 1971, word was received that Sergeant John Young was being transferred from the Walter Reed facility in Bethesda, Maryland to the Veteran's Medical Center Hospital in Manchester, New Hampshire where he would continue his extensive rehab procedures on an outpatient basis. Thank God, thought John. It's time for me to get on with the rest of my life.

With stabilization fully achieved, it was time for him to leave Bethesda, Maryland and head home. It was determined that he could be transported by automobile which meant a family member could drive him home. His call to Cathy telling her the good news was received with both sighs and tears. Of course, she would come down to drive him home. John suggested that maybe his Dad and her Dad could take care of that chore and she could stay at home with the baby. Reluctantly Cathy agreed to that suggestion and a date and time for pickup was tentatively agreed upon. Next Monday would be a wonderful day in the Young-Greco family circle. John would be home with Cathy and Colleen and his family and friends.

CHAPTER 6

The trip home was uneventful. Lots of good conversation between the men and a real time for bonding. John was brought up to date on all the happenings in Manchester, the things going on at the Locomotive Factory, Cathy's job at the Credit Union, how the baby had grown so fast and so much more.

It was close to four on Monday afternoon when the car entered the city limits of Manchester. It was still bright enough for John to view the town he loved and had so missed. It was almost two years since he had left.

As the car pulled into the driveway of the Greco home, John was quick to spot Cathy and Colleen as they came toward the car. There were other people around, but he was focusing on his immediate family.

John exited the car by himself. He was immediately clutched by Cathy who was holding their daughter, Colleen. A very meaningful embrace lasted for several minutes while they hugged each other and whispered their collective feelings. Amid the applause from those around John, he spotted his Mom and Dad and his sisters. They were with the Grecos and many friends of both John and Cathy who were there to celebrate the day. All in all, it was a wonderful day and he was so happy.

The remainder of the day passed quickly. Cathy sensed that John was getting tired. She decided that it was time for the party to be over and suggested that John needed to get some rest after his long trip home and all the excitement of the day. John was finally home now and would have plenty of time to catch up on all the happenings while he had been away. Visitors were quick to understand her urgency and said their goodnights rather rapidly. Within about five minutes the Greco home was vacant except for John and Cathy and their beautiful baby daughter Colleen.

Thank God, the Youngs had suggested that the Cathy's Mom and Dad might want to stay with them in Derry for a few days. Now it was time for a loving reunion and some sorely needed relaxation. John and the whole family slept very well that first night home.

PART THREE

READJUSTING TO CIVILIAN LIFE

Weldon James

CHAPTER 1

John and Cathy had so many things to consider that a sizable amount of their time was spent trying to prioritize those "to do" things by their importance and urgency. John had to go to the Veteran's Hospital in Manchester to start his rehabilitative therapy. This Hospital would be his base of operations for the rest of his life and he knew he had to establish himself with them quickly. The paperwork from Walter Reed had already been sent to the Hospital. John decided he would go there before the end of the week.

He was already receiving calls from his buddies at the Locomotive Company in Manchester. He figured he would go back and talk with people in the Personnel Department to see if there were any jobs that might be available for him, considering his handicap. He remembered a small staff that worked in the office, some were buyers and some were sales employees, for the Company. If he was lucky, he might be able to get a job with one of those groups. Only time would tell!

Cathy was returning to her job at the Credit Union while her Mom looked after Colleen. Over a short period of time, a semi-regular routine was starting to surface in their lives.

Cathy and John realized that it was not in everyone's best interest to continue to live at home with her parents. They had been most supportive of John and Cathy but now it was time to start to look for a place of their own. John's parents offered their place. However, before becoming a burden to anyone else in the family they decided to "go it on their own." Renting had been discussed. However, the thought was to buy a home if they could find what they wanted and more importantly, if they could afford it. This would become one of their top priorities and they agreed that they needed to start to look soon.

Settling in an apartment as they had done before was a consideration. However, they agreed that bringing up Colleen in her own home would be best for her and they dismissed the rental idea. This meant that they were going to spend some serious time investigating the local real estate market to see what was available and something they could afford.

They soon found that there were several new start-up neighborhoods within a radius of five miles of Manchester. Weekends would be the optimum time for looking. After several trips to view homes for sale and seeing nothing that appealed to them, they spotted an ad in the Manchester Union Leader that advertised a new development in the Bedford area.

John and Cathy set next weekend as the date for a trip to look at things in Bedford. The ad seemed to indicate the area was just being developed and all the homes that are for sale were just built. "Sounds like a starter neighborhood to me," remarked John.

On the following Saturday morning, the newspaper stated that there was an open house in Bedford that afternoon from 1P.M. to 3P.M. Cathy said, "I can't wait to see this area." Shortly after noon they left for the open house.

The area they saw was just beautiful. There were several Cape Cod style homes in addition to ranches, split level homes, and two or three colonials. Each home was surrounded by property that provided an ample feeling of privacy. It looked like some families had already moved in as they observed a few children playing in their backyards and several young adults outside planting shrubs and flowers.

After driving the area several times, they pulled into the open house to talk with the real estate person on duty. They discovered that there were several lots yet to be developed that were available, in addition to the homes that were ready. The prices seemed to be something that they could work with assuming they could obtain a mortgage. They retrieved a business card after leaving their names and contact information with the realtor and headed home to Colleen.

Surprisingly, the ride home was very quiet, as each one was mentally digesting the meeting with the real estate person and the impact of the action they might be about to take. Everything that they had observed met the criteria that they had agreed upon, even the lovely elementary school that was right there in the neighborhood.

Weldon James

CHAPTER 2

John had his first visit with the rehab people in the Manchester Veteran's Hospital. They had received his medical information from Walter Reed and were preparing the regimen that John would be receiving for the foreseeable future. It would be a slow but arduous routine that ultimately should provide more flexibility as John continues to heal. He would start with a visit of three days a week for now. His adapting to the therapy and observations of its effect on him would determine his future scheduling.

Before leaving Manchester, John decided to stop at the Manchester Locomotive Company to see if he could possibly return as an employee but in a different capacity. Obviously, he could no longer do the physical things that were a part of the job when he worked there last. A meeting with the Personnel Department could tell what might be available for him. Anyway, it would be a way to say hello to all those people he had worked with in the past.

John was greeted at the door by many of his fellow employees. After the brief encounter with his buddies, John was led into the Personnel office where he talked with the manager about job opportunities. After about a half hour, John was told that he would hear from the Company very shortly. With that information, John exited the Company and headed back to the Lake and his family.

On Saturday, the Grecos had planned a party and had invited the Youngs in addition to other friends. It was supposed to be a relaxing day to include a big barbeque and boat rides in the Greco's pontoon boat. The weather forecast indicated it would be a lovely sunny day with low humidity.

John's Mom, Dad, and sisters arrived on the early side to help the Grecos set up the picnic area. Other folks started arriving at about two o'clock and within a short period of time the party was in full swing.

The day passed so quickly. People started to leave about eight o'clock that evening, after spending some time roasting marshmallows by the fire pit. Everyone commented about what a wonderful day it had been and how happy they were to see John home and up and about.

Clean up took about twenty minutes. Both families were sitting on the patio when John and Cathy thought it might be a good time to mention their trip to the Bedford area looking at starter homes under construction and for sale.

"We want to tell you about something Cathy and I have been doing during the past several weeks," commented John. "We have been looking at new starter homes over in the Bedford area. There are ranches and split levels and even a few colonials. They look like they are well built and that a great new neighborhood is developing in that town. Most of the people we saw were young and some had children with them."

Cathy chimed in with her observations. "A short commute for both John and I to the Veteran's Hospital in Manchester would be great. There is a new elementary school down at the end of the neighborhood which would be a wonderful place for Colleen to go to when she is ready. All in all, this appears to be an area that would allow us to start to develop a closer relationship with our neighbors and one that would free up the house for you, Mom and Dad. You have both been so good to us and we appreciate it so much. Now may be the time to go it on our own, settle down and create a family homestead for ourselves, Colleen and her soon to be brother or sister."

Suddenly the silence was broken when the Grecos asked the obvious question, "Are you pregnant Cathy?"

"Yes, Mom and Dad, we just found out yesterday! I'm due next April."

After the customary congratulations, the Grecos and the Youngs tried to digest the news about Cathy and the overall effect it might have on all the families. Right now, John didn't even have a job.

Weldon James

CHAPTER 3

It was about nine thirty on that bright Thursday morning when the phone rang out at the Lake. It had been about seven or eight days since John had stopped at his old stomping grounds, the Manchester Locomotive Company to see if he could get a job there. After all, he had been successively employed there before being drafted and going off to war. Maybe this was the call he was waiting for since he had received nothing in the mail.

"Hello," said John.

"Good morning John," said the female voice on the other end of the line. "This is Debbie from Manchester Locomotive. We were wondering if you would be available to meet with Bruce Compton, our Plant Manager, tomorrow morning at ten?"

After a few seconds of silence, John replied that he was available and would be there tomorrow morning. He thanked Debbie for the call. His mind raced with many thoughts of what he might expect tomorrow. Thank God, perhaps he was at least being considered to return to work again at the Manchester Locomotive Company.

John immediately called Cathy to tell her the good news followed by a call to his parents. Besides playing with Colleen, John had become the best diaper changer in all New Hampshire. He also had mastered the art of feeding Colleen and burping her to release all the gas that usually comes with feeding followed by a nap. That was the normal daily routine. It didn't get much better than this.

Later he and Cathy talked about the possibility of his return to work and that they felt that they could rely on Cathy's Mom to baby-sit, at least at the beginning. Of course, with both having jobs and a secure future, they could now pursue the possibility of buying that first home. After the supper that John had prepared, they curled up on the couch and watched some early evening TV.

The next morning came all too early, but it didn't take long to realize the importance of just what was going to happen that day. Cathy finally headed off to work while Lucy administered to little Colleen. John was dressed and ready to leave the Lake and meet with Bruce Compton down at the factory. He borrowed one of the Greco cars and was on his way.

John parked in the visitor's parking spot and was soon climbing the front steps to enter the headquarters building. It was 9:55 A.M. according to his watch, which meant he was on time. He entered the Personnel Office and was greeted by Debbie. He was offered a chair while Debbie called upstairs for Bruce. Within five minutes, the door opened and Bruce Compton, who looked to be in his early fifties, entered the room. He and John shook hands and left for Bruce's office.

One thing Bruce noticed was that John had given him a firm handshake which is something that is looked at positively by those in the business. John felt comfortable with Bruce but didn't like his choice of suspenders. Oh, well!

John and Bruce talked for about an hour before the interview ended with Bruce inviting John to have lunch with him. He suggested a small diner about five minutes away and said he would drive. John agreed, and they walked outside to Bruce's car. Bruce felt it was important to see how John handled himself in a social environment. Was he conversant, did he display confidence, did he easily fit in or was he too reserved and not outgoing enough to portray the normal buyer type characteristics. Being a controlled extrovert would really fit the job and its description. Conversation with John had already produced the fact that he knew the product and could freely talk about its production and capabilities. He seemed relaxed in having a conversation and could express himself without any grammatical mistakes. After all, he was going to be representing the Company and needed to be everything the Corporation needed to have to succeed.

After lunch, Bruce drove back to the plant and thanked John for coming in and for having lunch with him. He indicated he would be hearing from the Personnel Department very soon. John thanked Bruce for the interview and lunch and said his farewell.

It wasn't long before he was pulling into the driveway out at the Lake and putting closure on the stressful day he had just experienced. I wonder which way it will go thought John, as he picked up Colleen and held her close.

Weldon James

CHAPTER 4

At precisely ten, the next morning, the phone rang at the house on the Lake. John, who was up attending to his daughter, made his way to the phone and said "hello."

After a second of silence the voice on the other end of the line identified herself as Debbie calling again from the Locomotive Company. John's heart seemed to skip a beat as he wondered what he might hear from Debbie. Was there more to the interview process or was this just a thank you for coming in yesterday, but the job had been given to someone else? Debbie asked if John were available that afternoon at two, to meet once more with Bruce Compton. John said he could make the arrangements to be at the factory that afternoon and thanked Debbie for the call. Hooray!

John asked Nora, the neighbor next door, out at the Lake to watch Colleen since Cathy's Mom was out shopping and probably would not be home until later that afternoon. Nora said "sure," which freed John up for his second interview with Bruce Compton. Finally, something was going right and all he could do was hope that something positive came out of this second meeting with Mr. Compton.

John entered the Locomotive Company at 1:45 P.M. to have his next meeting with the Plant Manager. Debbie, recognizing John, reached for her desk phone and alerted Bruce Compton's office that John had arrived. Within about two minutes, Bruce Compton appeared and shook John's hand once again. He suggested that they go to his office and continue their conversation. John smiled and wondered if he was going to be told that he had not met the requirements for the job.

After entering his office, Bruce asked John to have a seat in front of his desk. John thought, here it comes.

Bruce started the conversation by indicating to John that the Company was very interested in his return to work based upon his past work and abilities. Bruce also mentioned that he was aware that John had a long commitment with the Veteran's Hospital in Manchester which could be problematic for anyone to be in the sales end of the business. Bruce also recognized that the job that John had come from before being drafted required a certain amount of strength and manual dexterity which had been taken from John.

After a pause, Bruce stated that there was an opening for a buyer and that he thought that it would be a natural for John. It meant no overnight travel or trips to trade shows. It meant that he would be available to visit the Veteran's Hospital when he needed to and that he could be home evenings with his wife and soon to be larger family.

Tears filled John's eyes as he looked away for a second and then back to Bruce. He stood and extended his hand to Mr. Compton, thanking him for the opportunity and for the job. His tears didn't go unnoticed by Bruce. John was directed back to the Personnel Office to fill out some new paper work and to sign his new contract. He once again, thanked Bruce for his support and for his new job.

John was instructed to report to Dave Gilman who was the head buyer for Manchester Locomotive. Dave would teach him all about the nuances of buying and be his new boss. John remembered hearing Dave's name before from his Dad and what a nice guy he was. He looked forward to next Monday morning when his new life at Manchester Locomotive would begin.

One of Life's Journeys

On his way home, John thought just how happy and lucky he was. A war behind him, a lovely wife, a beautiful daughter, a new job and expert medical care. How lucky could one get!

PART FOUR

LIFE IN BEDFORD HILLS

Weldon James

CHAPTER 1

The Youngs started to spend available weekend time in the Bedford area looking for their new home. It was so exciting to be together and to be house looking for their family's first residence. The area was lovely. All new style homes, all with some property to enjoy, all with what appeared to be young families and plenty of kids. A school had recently been built to accommodate the expected influx of new families and was very close to all the property being developed. The closeness of the development to their work locations really made the entire effort a winner.

Now came the time for a major decision. What style do we want and where in the community should we build? They finally saw a piece of property on a cul-de-sac, that when built upon would be perfect for them and the kids. They returned to the onsite real estate office and met with an agent who would be happy to help them with their selection. After many questions and answers, they finally came to an agreement to buy a three-bedroom split level home with a two car garage to be built on Lot# 9 on the White Birch Drive cul-de-sac. The home would be ready for occupancy within three months from the date of the contract signature. The contract was signed, and a deposit given to the agent.

The Youngs immediately returned to the cul-de-sac and fantasized together about how happy they would be there and of all the things they could do together as a family. Now it was time to leave and tell everyone about their wonderful decision.

The ride back to the Lake was rather quiet as each one of them were digesting what had just happened and the impact it would have on their future as parents, neighbors and workers.

CHAPTER 2

As soon as construction started, many weekend trips were made to Bedford to witness the progress of what would soon become their family home.

The three months passed very quickly and before they knew it, they were meeting with the contractor to select the final touches, before the closing on the property. They were able to secure the necessary mortgage to complete the deal and had their closing on a Thursday afternoon in an Attorney's office in Manchester. The Youngs had contracted for movers to take care of their relocation the Monday following the closing. That Monday night was the first time they slept in their new home.

Construction had been going on at many other sites and completions of contracts were happening every week. People were moving into their new homes as quickly as possible. It didn't take long for the neighborhood to automatically begin to develop.

Meeting new people was an evening thing that happened throughout neighborhood as people walked after supper. A new family named Crown suggested that the neighborhood start an association.

Bob Crown was talking up the idea and decided on his own to approach the principal at the newly built elementary school in the neighborhood. The school administration was asked if the people from the "new neighborhood" would be able to use the auditorium on a weeknight for about a two hour block of time to discuss organizing as a neighborhood association. The local Board of Education responded affirmatively, and a date was set for the meeting. Tuesday evening, November 3rd at 7 P.M., was the date agreed upon.

CHAPTER 3

Bob Crown was starting to be recognized as a leader by neighbors and had their support to have a neighborhood meeting. He also had started a list of names and telephone numbers of his neighbors so if someone needed help they could contact him. Bob bought a supply of post cards and notified all the new neighbors of the meeting time and place and the purpose for the meeting. These were placed in all the mail boxes in the area.

On the meeting night, there were over seventy five people in attendance. Bob Crown asked for everyone's attention as he started to share his vision for the needs of a recognized association in their newly developed area. One of the new neighbors, who was in attendance, identified himself as a practicing attorney. He agreed with Bob Crown and indicated he would research other association bylaws and would like to be a part of the effort. After a lot of interesting conversations, Bob decided to ask for a show of hands of those in the room who thought forming an association was a good idea. Almost every hand was raised in agreement. Bob closed the meeting stating that they would meet again soon after Bill Morris, the attorney, completed his survey. Bob and Bill discussed the neighborhood response as they were walking to their cars and decided that they would talk often as the association was being developed.

Cathy and John were happy that they had attended the meeting. Besides agreeing with the association concept, they had the opportunity of introducing themselves to many of their new neighbors.

In early December, a call to those that were at the original meeting, informed them that it was time to reconvene and hear about associations and what Bill had learned. The purpose of the evening after Bill's report, was to officially name their new association and to vote in a slate of officers who would represent the organization. They wanted to complete this part of the process before the Christmas holidays would take over everyone's interest and time.

They met again as a group on December 9th at the school. Those in attendance heard Bill's report. After questions were answered, a vote of the group produced Bob Crown as the newly elected President, Diane Mooney as Vice-President, John Young as Treasurer and Bill Morris as legal representative. The group decided to call their new association The Bedford Hills Association. The officers decided to meet right after the holidays to draft the By Laws and finalize the Constitution of the organization.

CHAPTER 4

Christmas in the Young's new home was a wonderful get together for both families. Santa was on display everywhere in the new neighborhood. A light snow covered the area and Santa did his thing.

A great meal was prepared by the grandmothers, Doris and Lucy. John's sisters were there to enjoy the holiday with their niece and of course the entire family. All in all, it was a great day but very tiring. The families finally left at about nine and the lights were out at the Young's home by ten.

New Year's evening came and went without any fanfare since the weather was acting up and Cathy, being pregnant, did not want to have anything happen to her. Finally, New Year's Day arrived and the holidays were coming to a quiet end.

It was 3:45 in the morning on April 6th when Cathy's "water" broke, and a call was placed to her Doctor. She was experiencing contractions about every five minutes. The Youngs were told to head to the Hospital in Manchester. On the way they dropped Colleen off at the Grecos and carefully drove to Manchester. Her contractions were about two minutes apart when they arrived.

John was in the waiting room when the Doctor approached to tell him that everything went very well and that he was the father of a healthy son. John was able to join Cathy and his new son, John Jr., within ten minutes. He was taken aback by his size and held him very carefully. He returned him to Cathy and John kissed them both. What a day this had been and it's just starting. Before leaving the hospital, he made the customary calls to both families telling them all about his new son and their new Grandson.

CHAPTER 5

Cathy had negotiated for a "leave of absence" when her new baby was born. The Youngs were now at home as a family and adjusting to a new family member. A routine started to develop as time started to pass. There were times when Cathy would rely on John's help. This was usually in the evenings when he was home from work and available to change diapers and rock little Johnnie to sleep. During one of those evenings, Cathy and John agreed that the baby would be called Jack, instead of Junior or John, which would have produced confusion in years to come.

On April 13th, Bob Crown called for the newly elected officers of the Association to meet at his house at 7 P.M. The agenda was to discuss the new Association, construct some bylaws and to decide to seek Town recognition of the Association.

All were in attendance and on time. Membership would not be mandatory but strongly encouraged. A small stipend would be collected annually from the membership to support a neighborhood scholarship for a graduating senior high school student headed to college.

Certain rules were suggested that would keep the entire neighborhood looking as pristine in the future as it looked now. An example would be no one could construct a fence beyond the front of their house. Several rules were adopted by the officers and they would be presented at the next general meeting for neighborhood approval.

John and Dave Gilman, his new boss at the Locomotive Company, bonded very quickly and in a short period of time John knew what was expected of him and how to produce those results without anyone holding his hand. He became recognized as a competent asset to the Company who needed little supervision to get the job done.

During the next several months lots of things happened. John's Dad, Bob, retired from his many years with the Company. He was given a wonderful retirement party, in addition to his pension and benefits that he had earned over the past thirty plus years.

Three months after Bob Young's retirement, Dave Gilman, John's boss, announced his retirement. Within two days John was summoned to Bruce Compton's office. The Plant Manager had made his decision, and that decision was to promote John to head buyer at the Locomotive Company.

John was completely surprised by the promotion he just received. He thanked Bruce as a tear appeared in one of his eyes. Once in the car and on the way home, he reflected on what had just happened and that he would be responsible for making sure that all the buying efforts for the entire Company were professionally administered. He couldn't wait to tell Cathy and the parents. The new job also called for a nice raise that is always welcomed by a new young family. He thought, there truly is a God.

After phone calls to the parents, he and Cathy celebrated for the remainder of the evening.

During the remainder of that year Cathy and John were very busy with their family. She had negotiated an extended leave of absence from the Granite State Federal Credit Union which meant she could function as a stay at home Mom. Both she and John talked about there being an adult at home with the children as they started to grow up. They also had some time to develop close personal friendships with several of their neighbors.

The Association was heavily subscribed to which indicated to all that the neighborhood shared the same concerns and visions for its members. There were many neighborhood children attending the school, which ultimately became the central place for Association meetings. Many neighborhood functions had their start at the school. The executive committee met monthly in the beginning. Once a loose form of governance was put in place and agreed to at a full membership meeting, a calendar of upcoming events was addressed by those who volunteered to manage them. All in all, things were progressing very nicely with the Bedford Hills Association in Bedford, New Hampshire.

All too soon, the kids were students in the Bedford Hills Elementary School. With encouragement and support from their parents, they were doing very well. The holidays came and went with the normal school functions open to the families. The Greco and Young families had ample opportunity to observe their grandchildren in many school functions and took full advantage of those opportunities.

One summer, several close friends of Cathy and John suggested that they have a special cookout for several families. It was agreed on and everyone involved got to work on their part of the effort. John suggested the party be at their house right outside the patio in the yard. A rain date was discussed and agreed upon if the first date got rained out.

The special cookout was going to be unique. It included digging a pit in the backyard, three foot deep. The pit had to be about four foot square. Chris Jones and a new neighbor, Sam Taylor, accepted the responsibility. Next was lining the pit with stones about as big as grapefruits. This included the bottom and the sides all the way up. A wooden fire needed to be started in the pit 24 hours before the cookout. Keeping the fire going until cooking time was also important.

Two neighbors were sent to the shore to collect at least two barrels of fresh seaweed. Bob Crown and Bill Morris won that assignment. Two more neighbors were sent to buy many fresh, live lobsters and several dozen ears of corn to feed the participants. They could also secure some beef products for those who don't like lobster. Jim Archer and his wife Ann volunteered to get the food. Everyone couldn't wait for Saturday afternoon which was picnic day.

Finally, Saturday came and it was time to assemble the goodies and start cooking. The fire had been heating the stones all night and they all had a white hue. First thing was to layer the bottom of the pit with several inches of seaweed. This drew a small crowd since no one had ever experienced this type of cooking before. This was John's job. He then spread a layer of live lobsters and covered them with a layer of seaweed. He repeated the layering process until all the lobsters were in the pit. Next, he layered the pit with corn still in its husk. The last layer would be whatever seaweed was left. The pit was covered with a tarp. Everyone had to wait for several hours as the lobsters were being steamed in seaweed and the corn was being cooked in its husk.

The special cookout was a great success and the weather was perfect. Everyone raved about the party and suggested that it become an annual event.

John and Cathy were very tired after the party. They agreed with the fact that it should become an annual party, but next year someone else should host it. John felt a little weak the next morning but as the day progressed he felt his strength return.

Many conversations were held between those neighbors who had attended the party the night before, while they were cutting their lawns. After all it was Sunday morning and still part of the weekend.

CHAPTER 6

Regular neighborhood routines started quickly as the development was completely sold out. Most buyers were young families, some with small children. Those with school age children found that the school was providing an excellent education for their kids and all were happy with the time and effort spent by the faculty to teach.

As time passed Colleen and Jack had become students and were participating in many school presentations. Cathy had returned to work part time. Help from the two sets of grandparents on two weekdays managing the children after school, provided the opportunity to earn some additional funds for the Young family. She had started bank accounts for the children which someday would become valuable assets for them to have.

John quickly adapted to his new job as head buyer for the Company. Bruce Compton was sure to keep John in the loop and commended him on his excellent job performance. John was still visiting the Veteran's Hospital in Manchester. He was responding to his physical therapy on schedule and did not seem to be in any pain. However, he would still feel fatigued at times and recently had a spell of night sweats and a stomach ache. It all went away the next morning, so he didn't give much thought to the episodes.

That summer, the Young family and the Crown family and their kids spent two weeks at the shore. They had rented a large home right on the water at Hampton Beach. What a great fun time it was for the whole group.

John developed a severe headache on Thursday of the second week. On Friday he felt weak and lousy. Saturday morning came quickly and that meant the trip back to Bedford and reality. John drove and was feeling better, which made Cathy feel better, since she had been aware of his earlier discomfort down at the shore. John had decided that on his next trip to the Veteran's Hospital he would mention how he had been feeling lately. He was due for an appointment in about three months.

Soon the summer days would come to an end and the kids would be returning to school. The family routines, or lack of routines, would change. Fall in New Hampshire was a beautiful time to take in nature as it paints a beautiful picture of the changing season that all too soon would be with them. Neighborhood functions were being planned for the children and savored by the adults.

The Bedford Hills Association was up and running as designed. Over ninety percent of the families living in the "Hills" were members whose mantra was keep it neat, keep it clean and keep it safe. The Executive Committee met bi-monthly to discuss any problems and to constantly review the rules of the community as agreed upon by the Association members.

PART FIVE

REALITY

CHAPTER 1

As fall came and winter was approaching, John was experiencing more and more types of discomfort. He had contracted a cold that took a long time to abate and, on occasion, he would feel somewhat tired at work. One day Cathy asked John whether he was trying to lose some weight since she started to notice a drawn appearance, particularly in his cheeks. He responded he hadn't weighed himself in many months but would do so the next morning. The next morning provided a surprise for John when he found that he was down about seventeen pounds from his last weighing. Maybe a call to the Veteran's Hospital was appropriate instead of waiting for his scheduled appointment.

John made that call the next morning from work. He was given an appointment for Friday at 11 o'clock in the morning. The apprehension of waiting and worrying started to take its toll. What if I am sick with something, was foremost in John's mind. Well, Friday will tell!

John and Cathy passed a rather quiet week. The kids were always the focus of attention. They were adapting to school and constantly talked about the kids in their classes. The week passed quickly.

On Friday morning Cathy and John arrived at the Veteran's Hospital at about 10:45 A.M. and started the check in procedure. They were ushered into the attending Doctor's office at 11:00 A.M. sharp. Dr. Miller performed the usual office visit routine while John was discussing his physical ability to perform normal duties. Toward the end of the visit John mentioned the changes in how he felt. The Doctor questioned the length of time that John had been experiencing these feelings. John responded by saying for over a year but that they were coming more often. The Doctor asked John to describe the feelings. John responded by saying he felt tired some of the time, that he had the night sweats several times, occasional headaches, a cold that lasted a long time and that he was losing weight.

CHAPTER 2

The Doctor requested that John go to the laboratory for a blood testing sample and that he would hear back from him as soon as the results were ready. John and Cathy thanked him and stopped at the Lab before they exited the building for their trip back home. Little conversation meant that individually they were attempting to digest just what happened and what the outcome might be. They were sure that they would hear next week.

They had a big weekend planned, what with Halloween and all. The kids were so excited and were looking to play trick or treat with their friends as they canvassed the neighborhood.

The weekend passed without incident and soon it was Monday morning again. The kids were ready for school and John was ready for another day with the Locomotive Company. Today was important since he had several appointments with vendors which usually lasted into the early evening hours. Still no word from the Doctor. In this case, no news was considered good news.

The next morning at 9:45, John's office phone rang. It was a call from his Doctor. Dr. Miller requested that John come in to see him after work. John agreed to stop by. The afternoon proved to be an anxious one as John pondered the call to his office and what the Doctor might say. It obviously had to do with the results of the lab test from last week.

John left work a little on the early side and entered the Veteran's Hospital at about 4:45 P.M. He went directly to Dr. Miller's office and waited for the Doctor to come out and acknowledge his presence. Finally, the door opened and Dr. Miller motioned for John to come into his office. He was guided to a chair in front of the Doctor's desk and the meeting began.

Dr. Miller stated that the results of the blood samples had come back. He indicated that an abnormality was detected and that he wanted to have the lab work repeated to be sure that the original results were accurate. John immediately asked what the first test had shown. After a minute, Dr. Miller replied that the first test had shown an elevated white cell count in his blood and that there was a chance that John might have leukemia. Dr. Miller stated that the symptoms John had mentioned earlier coincided with those experienced by patients diagnosed with leukemia.

John couldn't believe what he just heard. My God, what happens to me now? He immediately thought of Cathy and the kids and what may be the future for them if the second test confirmed the findings of the first test and if he couldn't beat this terrible disease. John asked the Doctor what the options were in treating this disease. Dr. Miller said he would be prepared to talk more with John after the new results were posted. John left the Doctor's office and headed to the Lab for his second blood drawing.

The walk back to the car was frightening. God Almighty, what the hell do I do now? John's mind raced as he drove home where he was met at the door by Cathy. She immediately knew something was wrong when she saw that John had been crying, as evidenced by the redness of his face and the moisture on his cheeks. After entering their home, John grabbed Cathy and held her close as he told her what Dr. Miller had told him. She burst into tears as they both held each other as tightly as they could. After several moments of silence, John said that they would get the results of the second test on Thursday. That equated to two more days of terrible anxiety and worry. They both agreed that they would not tell the parents until after the results were known. No need to get them all upset before a final diagnosis was reached.

On Thursday morning, John was called by the Doctor to come back to the office at the Veteran's Hospital. John and Cathy left for the ride to Manchester. Once there, they immediately went to the office and were greeted by the secretary who ushered them into the Doctor's office. Dr. Miller stood and suggested that they sit down in front of his desk as he seated himself behind his desk.

"John, the results of the second test confirm the results of the first test. You do have a form of leukemia that is creating the symptoms we had discussed. Your leukemia has been diagnosed as Chronic Lymphocytic Leukemia. With the right types of treatment, we can possibly get this thing into remission. I want to get started with a medicine that is part of the field of chemotherapy. That coupled with possible blood transfusions may bring this thing under control. It will mean setting a schedule that requires you to be here on an outpatient basis several times a week. Blood transfusions may be introduced as we follow the results of the chemotherapy."

John was told that his first appointment was the following Monday morning at ten. Cathy and John knew that many questions were left unsaid as they rather slowly drove home. They discussed when the parents should be told. They decided to invite them over on Sunday for dinner and tell them then. Keeping the seriousness of the situation from the children at this time was also agreed upon. There was certainly no need to have them worry about Daddy, if they heard he was sick.

CHAPTER 3

Sunday afternoon at the Young's house was an event that those in attendance wouldn't soon forget. Both sets of parents arrived at about the same time. At approximately 4 o'clock John asked everyone to meet in the living room. As they sat down, Doris Young wondered whether this was going to be an announcement that she was going to be a Grandmother again.

John started the conversation by stating that he had just returned from the Veteran's Hospital with some concerning news about himself. It seems that he has been diagnosed with Chronic Lymphocytic Leukemia which will require a massive amount of treatment time in hopes that it will go into remission.

After a moment of silence by the parents, as they tried to digest just what John had conveyed to them, the inevitable questions from everyone started. Doris started to cry as did Lucy, Cathy's Mother. The scene was very somber while John tried to answer all their questions as intelligently as he could. Where in hell did this come from and why did it happen to John, thought Bob, John's Dad. Joseph Greco just sat in silence, shaking his head in utter disbelief. My God, what will Cathy do now, was his initial thought.

Both sets of parents, who were obviously shaken by this news, mentioned that they were here for their children and grandchildren and would help in any way they could. This meant taking the kids any time, babysitting, shopping for the family and anything else that was needed. John and Cathy thanked them.

101

John finally commented that it was now time for dinner and a change of subject. Silent agreement was obvious, as the parents nodded their heads, and headed toward the dining room table. The kids came in from outside, washed their hands and the family sat down to a very unusual Sunday get-together. The kids kept the conversation going as the parents were still reflecting on the report that they had just heard.

After dinner the grandmothers got the kids ready for bed since there was school the next morning. Shortly after nine that evening, the parents left John and Cathy's house, still with so many thoughts and questions in their minds.

Once at home, they would do as much research as they could to try and understand this dreaded disease. The Manchester Public Library would certainly be on their list of places to look first. No one experienced a good night's sleep that night.

The next morning, John called the office and said he would be delayed that morning but would be there after noon. As he drove to the Veteran's Hospital, he wondered what they were going to do to him when he arrived. John was ushered back into Dr. Miller's office. The Doctor was going to brief John on the treatments he would be receiving to try to get the leukemia into remission and hopefully cured. His first treatment would be several doses of chemotherapy which is designed to kill the bad cells. There would be ongoing blood testing during this phase of treatment to see if the chemotherapy was effective in attacking the errant cells. Also, blood transfusions were available to stabilize a very high white cell blood count. John was made aware that he may feel very ill by receiving these treatments and possibly lose his hair. Once again, constant blood testing would be part of his regimen to assess the effects of the therapy.

John couldn't believe what he had just heard. My God he thought, this may be a tough time but I'm going to beat this son of a bitch.

John had his first chemotherapy infusion that day and went to work that afternoon. He asked to talk to Bruce Compton and met with him in his office at 4 P.M. John told Bruce the whole story and that he hoped he would be able to continue his work while undergoing the treatments. Bruce assured John that he would have all the time he needed to receive his therapy and he was sure that John would beat this thing.

John felt better about the whole thing as he headed home to Cathy and the kids. It'll be a struggle but I'm going to lick this damn thing.

That evening after the kids went to bed, John filled Cathy in on what he had to look forward to in the future. Cathy had been to the library that day, while the kids were in school, and researched the type of leukemia that John has and the medicines available to treat it. She also read about the reactions to chemotherapy and the dietary considerations that go with that type of treatment. Cathy told John of her trip to the library and what she had learned. He teared up and held her close.

How lucky was he to have a wonderful person like Cathy who would research the disease and try to help in every way she possibly could to support him and what he may look forward to. A small glass of wine for each of them soon put them to sleep.

Weldon James

CHAPTER 4

John reacted very well to his first chemotherapy sessions and had been able to withstand the obviously dramatic side effects of using chemo as a protocol. He experienced nothing that would keep him from continuing his normal work routine at the Locomotive Company or even a normal life style at home. When could he look forward to stopping the medication and how soon would he know if it was successful and he was in remission, or even cured? These questions haunted him daily. He was sure they were shared by just about everyone who was going through the same types of procedure. When will this terrible thing be over?

John followed his routine for injections for the length of the first application schedule. A blood test showed a slight improvement in the number of red blood cells and a lessening of the while cell count. This was an indication that the chemo was having a positive effect in trying to stem the progress of the disease.

During the protracted treatment schedule John had been living as normal life, as he could. There were school events that he and Cathy attended, neighborhood meetings that he, as treasurer, attended and many other social functions that they both participated in without any apparent discomfort on John's part. The only noticeable change was that John was starting to lose his hair and go bald.

Colleen was now a great student and had many local friends that she went to school with. They played together on weekends since they were good friends and classmates living only two blocks apart. There were always birthday parties that were filled with many kids from the neighborhood.

Cathy and John Young and Jenny and Bill Hunter were members of the neighborhood association and had become close friends. The Hunters had two children, Gerald, who was called Jerry, and a daughter, Ann. Both of their kids were in the same school as the Youngs and all played together. The kids became very close over the years as they matured. It was like a large family.

Jenny and Cathy had started a book club that had seven members who met at a different home every month. Their husbands would get together on occasion, but most of the time they were relegated to baby-sitting their kids. They would, however, find the time in the summer with several other neighbors to go trout fishing on occasional weekends in upper New Hampshire. They always bought the catch home and had a fish fry at someone's home.

All during this time John was going for treatments and having blood tests to determine if there were changes in his condition and just how his body was reacting to the therapy. On several occasions, he was given some time off from his Hospital routine because the blood tests had shown an improvement in starting to help stop the spread of the disease. Even though this wasn't a recognized form of remission, John always wanted to believe he was on the way to a full recovery. Psychologically this helped him cope with the daily thought processes that haunted his everyday being.

CHAPTER 5

During the next three years the Young children grew and matured as all other neighborhood kids did. Many friendships were generated that would last no matter where people finally wound up living.

John had adjusted to his medical routine without a great deal of difficulty and seemed to be responding to his therapy with some ease. The only sign of any problem was that he had lost all his hair, but everyone who knew John knew why. After all, there were a lot of naturally bald young men around, so only those familiar with the family knew the real reason. There were months that would go by when the blood tests were stable enough for John to stop the regimen. The Doctors at the Veteran's Hospital were reluctant to call the results of several blood tests a form of remission. However, they seemed to be positive when discussing the results of all the tests with John. This obviously made him feel better about the whole situation. He couldn't wait for the remission call and ultimately the all clear sign.

John, Cathy and the kids attended John's sister Amy's wedding in June of that year. Colleen was asked to be the flower girl and did a fine job. Everything went as expected and the entire family enjoyed all the pomp and circumstance that usually accompanies a family wedding. John and Cathy were fond of Mark Plante, their new brother-in-law. They had met him a year ago and were happy for Amy and Mark as they made their commitment to each other. Downside, the new Mr.

and Mrs. Plante were moving to New York City, where they both had jobs. Upside, it was a place that they could go for a visit from time to time, while John's condition was under control.

Visits to the Veteran's Hospital for treatment, always preceded by blood work, plus the history of where John had served while in the Army led the Doctors to suspect that he might have been exposed to Agent Orange. Agent Orange was a defoliant that was used around Army base camps to allow visual monitoring of select areas, usually associated with the paths that the enemy would use when attacking the camp from a dense foliage area. Its side effects have been associated with a suspected list of diseases including leukemia.

It was early in October when John had another bout with his illness. This one was severe enough for him to be admitted to the Hospital while he was undergoing treatment and trying to regain his strength. During this stay, it was established that, he was very probably the victim of exposure to the Agent Orange liquids. After all, he had been in a replacement Company awaiting assignment after arriving in Vietnam and had been assigned to assist in the unloading of all materials associated with war from the constant arrival of transport planes from the mainland. Several times the barrels of Agent Orange were dented, in some cases leaking and the fluid got on his hands. So much for the possible cause of the leukemia. Will it ever stop, went through John's mind on a daily basis.

It took about a week to stabilize John so that he could leave the Hospital and return to his family. While at the Hospital, John had many visits from not only the family but from many neighbors and co-workers. Everyone was praying for his recovery.

CHAPTER 6

During the next several months, John started to feel better and hoped the problem was in remission. John had been given some experimental medicines to see just what their effect on the disease would be. He seemed to be reacting favorably to the new protocols. His blood work showed an improvement and he generally felt good most days.

Time seemed to be racing by as the children grew and John's job became more complex. He now had four employees reporting to him. The business of buying had expanded as the construction of railroad engines became more demanding.

Neighborhood relationships had become an everyday part of their home life, not only between select adults, but their children. They had many things in common. They were all in the same age range. Most had kids attending the school right at the end of the neighborhood and many had relied on a neighbor for help from time to time. Good friendships were easily developed in the Bedford Hills neighborhood.

PART SIX

THE TRIP

Weldon James

CHAPTER 1

Since John seemed to be in remission, a fall vacation for he and Cathy was being planned. Paula Young, John's unmarried sister agreed to stay with her niece and nephew while their Mom and Dad were vacationing. It was going to happen after school had opened in the fall, which meant a lot of time would be spent in school and less time had to be utilized entertaining the kids. They were used to a regular routine and Aunt Paula would be there to only supervise the goings-on. It sounded like a plan!

Jenny and Bill Hunter, their best friends in the neighborhood, were asked by John and Cathy if they wanted to join them on their vacation. They immediately agreed. Both Jenny and Bill had negotiated the necessary time off from their jobs and were therefore available to go on a trip which amounted to a mini vacation.

After many evening meetings and a lot of investigation by both families it was agreed that they would go to Europe. The trip would last fourteen days and include a one-day river boat excursion on the Rhine River. This involved flying into Cologne, Germany and boarding a river cruise boat that would ultimately lead them to Wiesbaden, Germany, where they would rent a car for the rest of the trip. Their plan included being in Munich for the October Festival which happens during the last two weeks of September. They would then continue to travel to Berchtesgaden and Garmisch, Germany. The trip would end with a flight home from Salzburg, Austria.

The rest of the summer months were spent refining their trip plans and making their own reservations. Jenny had worked in a travel agency for several months and knew the routines to follow when developing a trip of this magnitude. If she was still working at the agency, she might have been able to negotiate some travel discounts.

There was unspoken concern whether John would be physically able to partake in the proposed trip. However, his doctors at the Veteran's Hospital had given him a green light to "go for it." This gave everyone a sense of relief that things would proceed as planned.

CHAPTER 2

The summer ended quickly, and it was now time that the children would be returning to school. Bill Hunter's Mother would stay with their kids, Jerry and Ann, while Aunt Paula was staying with the Young kids.

The scheduled date for departure was September 16th. They would be flying directly from Boston to Cologne, Germany. The airport was known as the "Cologne-Bonn" airport. Both families were packed for their trip by the 14th of September and ready to go.

The morning of the 16th of September was bright with no clouds to be seen anywhere. It was Sunday morning and both families went to church in Manchester. They had attended an early service since their flight departed at 5:30 that afternoon and they still had to drive to Boston to Logan Airport. Joe Greco was the designated driver.

After the customary hugs and kisses, the vacationers departed Bedford for Boston. They had to check in by four. The trip to Boston was uneventful and they were at the airport by 3:30 P.M. Joe Greco said his farewell and headed home.

Now all they had to do was wait until boarding. The flight on Lufthansa Airlines would arrive in Cologne the next morning at about 8:00 A.M. German time.

About one hour after being airborne, the flight attendants served drinks and took orders for dinner. After the meal was complete and the cabin cleaned up, the passengers had the option of listening to music or watching an up-to-date movie. Several seemed to doze early as the night flight continued. The Youngs and Hunters were dozing by 11 P.M.

They awoke as the light from the new day started to filter into the cabin of the plane. They were about an hour and a half from the airport in Cologne. People started to stir in the cabin and the lavatories were getting a work out, big time. The attendants were starting to serve coffee and rolls as the flight continued. At approximately 8:15 A.M. the plane landed at the airport. After collecting their luggage, they hailed a taxicab and went to their hotel.

They were staying at the Hotel Konigshof, which was located within walking distance of the center of town. Their rooms were small, very clean and comfortable. After a short readjustment to where they were, they decided to head downtown. They walked along the narrow store front lined streets, toward the end of town and toward the spires of the giant Cathedral of Cologne, which is located on the banks of the Rhine River. The spires were accessible if one wanted to climb over five hundred steps to view the whole countryside. In deference to John, they just toured the Cathedral from inside and were there when the church bells tolled the afternoon hour of three. A slow walk back to the Hotel, with time to browse the store windows, placed the group there at about 5:30 P.M.

John was visibly tired and wanted to go to their room before meeting for a drink and dinner in the hotel restaurant. He knew that after dinner and a possible short evening walk, they would all be retiring to their rooms to get some early sleep for the next day's early morning cruise on the Rhine River toward Weisbaden.

The next day they started a day long cruise on the River whose banks were festooned with grape arbors growing next year's wine for all to enjoy. They passed the remnants of the bridge at Remagen, which allowed the American 3rd Army to cross into Germany toward the end of World War II. The river had many turns and lots of river traffic, including barges loaded with coal. They continued toward the Hotel Nassauer Hof in Wiesbaden. They would stay there that night and rent a car the next morning as they proceeded toward Munich and the "Oktoberfest." That evening a traditional meal of sauerbraten and vegetables was thoroughly enjoyed by all.

The next morning after a German breakfast which included meats and cheeses, they rented a car for the rest of their trip. Bill was going to be the designated driver. The trip was going to be a long one. When realizing it was over 400 kilometers to Munich, they decided to split the distance and stay in Stuttgart for the evening. They secured rooms in the Hotel Rieker which took pressure off everyone on the trip, especially John, who up to this time, was feeling fine. They were able to have their meal at a restaurant located at the top of a giant communications facility that towered over the entire city. Leaving the next morning precluded them from visiting the popular Mercedes Museum located in Stuttgart.

After another day of driving, they finally entered the bustling city of Munich, which was originally the Capital of the State of Bavaria in the country of Germany. Their hotel was called the Drei Mohren and was located on the Shubertstrasse which was within easy walking distance of the entrance to the Oktoberfest. The Oktoberfest is held annually in a giant field area called Theresienwiese which is an area named after Theresa, the wife of Prince Ludwig of Bavaria. Another great plus to their hotel's location was the fact that the traditional Oktoberfest parade, which lasts about three hours, passes from downtown Munich right in front of their hotel on the way to the opening ceremonies.

Being able to sit in a chair on the balcony of their room on the second floor and observe the parade worked to John's advantage. He quickly recognized that each township in the State of Bavaria was represented by the local dress and special responsibilities. Those responsibilities included the growing of hops by everyone in a specific town or the hunters by every male in another specific town. Most were complete with their own marching band which certainly added to all the pomp and circumstance. Lastly, all the beer breweries in the whole area were represented in the parade, and were led in many cases, by their owners. It was quite a sight to see!

Later that afternoon the vacationers decided to go to the "Fest." However, after the parade, John had felt a little lightheaded, so they decided to take a break first. After all, the Fest was going to be there for another two weeks, so what's the hurry!

It was about 5 P.M. when they decided that the walk over to the Fest would not be a problem for John and they could get some German cuisine. The area was divided into two parts. Part one had all the prefabricated beer buildings with food and all the beer you could drink. Each building was loaded with picnic tables and had its own band which played all kinds of German music. Part two of the area was a giant amusement park with all sorts of rides and fun houses that appealed to almost everyone who was there.

In addition to the beer, they sampled the fried chicken, bratwurst, the Swiss cheeses with ground pepper and a large variety of German foods. It was a great evening enjoyed by all. At about ten o'clock, they thought it appropriate to head back to the hotel for some needed rest. John was starting to show some wear and tear as it was difficult for him to keep up with the group. Once back in their rooms, they could all relax and have a great discussion about their day's events and what they had observed.

CHAPTER 3

The next morning arrived too quickly, which meant it would soon be time to get started on another piece of their journey. After breakfast, they checked out of their rooms and headed out of town in their rented car.

A map provided by the hotel showed them how to avoid the morning rush hour in and around Munich. It was a great help in finding their way to the Alpine Highway that would lead them toward the Garmisch-Partenkirchen part of Bavaria. Two parts of this leg of the trip were interesting in that they would be able to visit a night club built by the American Army Engineers after the end of World War II as a recreation area for those service men awaiting repatriation home from Europe. Part two was a trip up the highest mountain in the German Alps and staying overnight in a German hotel located near the crest of the mountain.

The ride from the hotel in Munich was short when compared with other rides that they had experienced. Within a little over two and a half hours they were checking into the Golf-Hotel Sonnenbichl in Garmisch, Germany.

The first thing that caught their eyes was the local architecture of the buildings in this Alpine village. Noticeable was the fact that each window had a blooming flower box affixed to it. The exposed wooden framework shown on all their buildings was obvious and many buildings had painted murals on their outside walls. The streets were clean and easy to drive on.

Each couple decided that they would take a rest that afternoon before going out to their evening function. The concierge of the hotel was asked for a wake-up call at 5 P.M. Both calls came in within a minute of each other. John had fallen asleep, so this was a true wakeup call for him. The couples freshened up quickly and met in the lobby at about 5:30 that evening. The place they were going to was called the Casa Carioca. The desk clerk was able to give them directions and they went on their way.

The Casa Carioca was a combination restaurant and dancing venue in Garmisch that catered to American servicemen and women who were, or had been, in the service of their Country. The building outside was rectangular in shape and large enough in size to hold many patrons at the same time. To enter, one had to buy a ticket as though you were going to a movie theatre. The cost was only one dollar. Once inside they were led to dining tables that were situated on a series of indented levels above the dance floor, which was located down in the middle of the building. The inside of the building was shaped like a horseshoe with one end holding a giant stage with a large band playing soft dance music for the diners. The diners were on all levels with steps to go down to dance if they cared to.

Everyone was shocked to observe the prices for food and drink. Cocktails cost fifty cents each, while all highballs were forty cents each and all beer was thirty cents. Wines of a wide variety cost between a dollar and two dollars for a full bottle. What a night this could turn out to be! The dinner menu was even more inexpensive. Shrimp cocktail was seventy cents while a full filet mignon dinner was two dollars and twenty five cents. How could anyone go wrong with these prices, and you even had dancing!

About nine that evening, everyone heard a loud roaring noise as the dance floor down below started to move outside the building to expose a giant ice rink. The dance orchestra had been replaced by another band who started to play music as skaters from all over the lower level came onto the ice. An ice review that lasted two hours was then presented to all those in attendance.

Obviously, both couples were taken by surprise and amazed at what they had experienced with the meal, dancing, the prices and now a full ice show. It had been quite a night that wouldn't soon be forgotten.

John was exhausted when they got back to the hotel and went to bed immediately. Cathy, Jenny and Bill sat for a short time in the hotel lobby sipping a goodnight drink and discussing the day's activities. They all remarked about John and how he seemed to be holding up under the schedule and activities they were experiencing. They hoped that a good night's sleep might help him maintain his stamina. After all, the next day was going to be an exciting one also.

Several calls were placed home that evening. Everything sounded fine on the home front which made the vacationers feel good.

Weldon James

CHAPTER 4

After breakfast the next morning the foursome experienced a very short ride to a railroad station to board a train for the next part of their journey. They boarded the Bavarian Zugspitze Railroad which was a small train from Garmisch that headed toward the town of Eibsee. The trip was about fifteen minutes long. After taking on more passengers in Eibsee, the train left town and started to climb uphill. Looking out the window they could observe Lake Eibsee which was now below them. In a few more minutes the train came to a halt and the engine was disconnected. Another engine with the ability to climb a cog railroad had replaced the original engine. This engine was connected to the rear of the car and pushed the train all the way up the mountain. The views as they ascended the mountain were breathtaking.

The lake below seemed to get smaller as they climbed toward the top. About twenty minutes into the push up the mountain everything went black. The train was still climbing the mountain when it became obvious that they had entered a tunnel. About fifteen minutes later they arrived at their destination. The engine had pushed them right into the lobby of the hotel which was named the Schneefernerhaus. It was located near the top of the Zugspitze which is the highest mountain in the German Alps.

As the couples left the train, they couldn't help but view the snow laden peaks all around them. Some of the snow was somewhat grey in color since it had been there since last year and maybe for many years. They observed several cable car lines. One seemed to be going down the mountain while one seemed to be going further up the mountain. It didn't take them long to check in and go to their rooms to use the facilities. They all noticed that the air was quite a bit colder up here than down in Garmisch.

John was feeling a little lightheaded and decided to lay down for a while. Cathy, Jenny and Bill went to the desk to ask many questions. What time were lunch and dinner served, where was the bar, where do the cable cars go and finally how high above sea level were they? The desk clerk responded that they were 8100 feet above sea level, that one cable car goes to the summit which is just over 10,000 feet above sea level while one cable car goes back down to Lake Eibsee. He also indicated that lunch is served from noon until 2:30 and dinner is available from 6 P.M. until 9 P.M. The hotel bar is located down the hallway near the giant fireplace.

They thanked the clerk and headed to the bar for a celebratory drink. It was only one o'clock and they could still get lunch.

Once back in their room, Cathy asked John how he was feeling and if everything was all right. He commented that he felt very tired and had the sweats for no apparent reason. He also said that he felt weak. Cathy was concerned with his answers and hoped this was just a passing incident and that he would feel better after having some lunch.

They met the Hunters in the restaurant for lunch which consisted of sandwiches and a variety of soups. The first thing they noticed was that the prices at this hotel were much higher than the prices they had observed at the Casa Carioca.

"We have left the land of unbelievable prices and are back to the reality of commercial rates for our food and drink," commented Bill. Nodding heads displayed agreement with that comment.

John had a bowl of pea soup which seemed to make him feel better while the others sampled sandwiches and some soups.

After lunch, the group decided to take a cable car to the summit which supported a weather station and believe it or not, an Austrian Hotel. The border line between the countries was located at the summit. That way both countries could share the highest peak in the Alps.

They returned to their hotel about 5 P.M. just in time for a cocktail before dinner. John was starting to react to all the activity and the rareness of oxygen at that height above sea level. He seemed uneasy and was feeling a little lightheaded. He blamed these feelings on all the excitement of their new surroundings. After a cocktail laced with a lot of conversation by the four of them, they decided it was time for dinner.

They requested to be seated at a table near the fireplace, which was not only beautiful to observe, but also gave off some warmth to the room which was starting to get somewhat cooler with the dipping of the afternoon sun. The menu showed a small selection of offerings to select from. After discussion, the Youngs decided they would try the sauerbraten with cabbage and dumplings while the Hunters opted for the Hungarian goulash with spaghettis and a salad. They decided to split a bottle of Mosel-Riesling wine with their meal.

When dinner arrived, both couples gingerly sampled their dishes and found to their satisfaction that the food tasted great and was very filling. It didn't take long for the plates to be cleaned and conversation to resume. They discussed the dinner that they had just consumed and whether to follow it up with some desert. John passed while the others had a slice of black forest cake topped with a small scoop of vanilla ice cream. All agreed it had been a wonderful meal.

Since it was now just about 9:30 in the evening, they decided to go to their respective rooms and relax before going to bed and getting to sleep. After all, it had been a very active day for everyone and the rest could only help. In no time they were all sleeping and the night started to pass.

CHAPTER 5

It was about 4 A.M. when Cathy was awakened by hearing John coughing in the bathroom. It was as though he couldn't catch his breath. She got out of bed and went to him. He said he was having trouble catching his breath and felt very weak. Cathy immediately got him back to bed and called the front desk. After a long pause, an answer from the lobby was received. Cathy explained the problem and asked if there was a doctor in the hotel. The person in the lobby said "no" and asked if there was anything he could do to help. He suggested some oxygen might help since, on occasion, some clients have had a breathing problem at the height of the hotel above sea level. Cathy asked if some could be brought to their room and received an immediate answer of "yes."

Within minutes there was a knock on their door, which when opened, produced a person with a small portable tank of oxygen and a face mask for its use. It was immediately put on John's face and his breathing seemed to be somewhat relieved. However, he was very pale and seemed to be very weak.

Cathy called the main desk to ask about the earliest departure time they could leave the hotel considering they had arrived by cog railway, and there was no roadway nearby. The response was that there was an early morning trip down the mountain, on the first train leaving at seven. It was now close to 5:30 in the morning and she decided it was time to call the Hunters and tell them they were leaving on the 7 o'clock train and the reason for the change in itinerary. The Hunters were concerned and said they would be ready by that time and that Bill would be there to help John to the lobby and onto the train.

Jenny immediately called the desk and indicated that they were also checking out in the morning and would be on the 7 A.M. train with the Youngs. She also asked if the hotel could prepare some food for them to take as they took the trip down the mountain to Garmisch.

Cathy was back on the room phone again and further conversations with the front desk provided the name of a hospital in Garmisch and the fact that there would be taxi service at the train station in Garmisch when they arrived.

The Youngs and Hunters had checked out of the hotel and were patiently waiting for the train to depart. Bill had helped John to get somewhat comfortable in the rail car and all four were having a cup of coffee and a croissant as the train started to move.

John was visibly upset by the whole happening and was experiencing a real sharp headache. He only sipped the coffee and ate nothing from the platter that had been prepared for them by the hotel staff. When the train pulled into Eibsee, they all realized that in another fifteen minutes they would be in Garmisch, and John could get to a hospital. It couldn't be soon enough, thought John, as the train came to a halt in Garmisch.

It was time to get off and into a cab for the ride to the Garmisch-Partenkirchen Medical Center in Garmisch. The cab dropped them at the emergency room entrance and the group was met by the triage personnel.

CHAPTER 6

The hospital was very modern and large which meant that it probably covered a lot of the greater Garmisch area. Cathy immediately informed the emergency room doctor that her husband John was suffering from leukemia and had suddenly gotten ill up on the Zugspitze. An immediate call for blood work was made, and in what seemed to be only a few minutes a phlebotomist was on the scene, drawing blood from John's arm. The vials were then rushed to the hospital lab for analysis. Now all the Youngs and Hunters had to do was await the results. John seemed comfortable on the bed in the emergency room. He had been given an IV to help keep him hydrated.

Cathy, Jenny and Bill were waiting out in the hall and talking about what to do now. Cathy stated she thought it best for she and John to get home as soon as possible. The Hunters agreed, and Cathy decided that she would call the airline and try to effect a change in their itinerary.

She also knew that she had some important calls to make, alerting those at home as to what was happening. Bill offered to make calls to cancel the rest of the trip for all of them and help in any other way he could. Cathy decided to await the results of the blood work and diagnosis before calling home since it was still the middle of the night in New Hampshire. However, this was a good time to change plane reservations, if she could. Getting from Garmisch to Munich was another problem that had to be addressed.

She called Lufthansa Airlines and told them of her predicament and asked if there was availability on the next flight to Boston. The airline scheduler stated that there were only two seats available and those were in first class. Jenny, who was listening to the conversation, suggested Cathy grab them, and she and Bill would fly home on the next available flight. Cathy made the change.

While waiting for word from the doctor, Cathy decided to ask another question of the hospital staff. She asked if they had a medical helicopter as part of their equipment. She was surprised to find that they did. It apparently was used often when there were skiing accidents up on the mountains. She asked, if needed, could John be transported to the Munich airport from Garmisch. A hospital official said that if needed, they would transport John and Cathy to Munich. This meant that the Hunters would probably have to drive to Munich or take the train out of Garmisch to Munich. That decision would impact on their plans to return to the U.S.

Bill had finished his cancellation calls and was coming down the hall with hot coffee for the three of them. While sitting in the hallway, the emergency room doctor approached and gave the results of the blood work to the group. Apparently, John's white blood count was abnormally high, and he was in need of a blood transfusion as soon as possible to stabilize him. And yes, it looked as if he had had another bout with his leukemia and was no longer in any form of remission.

The doctor wanted to keep John in the hospital overnight to monitor him. This meant that Cathy and the Hunters would stay in Garmisch that evening and the departure for the Munich airport would happen the next morning. The helicopter departure time would get the Youngs to the Lufthansa terminal in plenty of time to catch the plane home.

Cathy spent some individual time with John telling him what they were going to do and when. He seemed more alert and vocal after the transfusion and was apologizing for what happened to him and the effect it had on everyone's vacation. He was told to stow that kind of conversation and just look at the brighter side of the fun that they had had up to that time. Soon he was dozing and Cathy, after kissing him goodnight, left the hospital. She cried all the way back to the hotel. However, the next duty that she must perform was going to be making those calls home that she knew would upset everyone.

Her first call was directed to the Youngs. It was about 9 A.M. in Manchester, New Hampshire. She had an operator at the hotel call the Young's residence for her.

"Good morning," Bob Young said, as he answered the phone.

Cathy immediately answered with "Hi, Mr. Young."

"How's the trip going?" he asked.

After a minute of silence Cathy responded, "Not too good, we have a problem. John is in the hospital here in Garmisch. He apparently has had a relapse and was really very sick last night. That's why we brought him to the hospital and they have given him a blood transfusion to help alleviate his symptoms and stabilize the situation."

Bob called for Doris to pick up a phone. Together they listened to Cathy retell the story. Cathy finally stated that they were coming home tomorrow since they had gotten two seats on a plane landing in Boston at four in the afternoon. She asked if Bob could pick them up and drive them to the Veteran's Hospital in Manchester.

Bob immediately replied, "We'll be there to get you tomorrow, honey. Please say hello to John for us. We'll be praying for you both."

Only two more calls to go and Cathy could at least lie down and try to get some rest, and if lucky, some sleep.

She called her Mom and Dad and told them the story. She indicated she would be back home tomorrow evening late and they could talk then. She told them that Bob Young was going to the airport to pick them up. After some additional conversation about the trip and what was going to happen to the Hunters, the call ended.

Her last call was to her home and to her sister-in-law Paula who was babysitting for the Youngs while they were on their trip. Paula was so upset to hear about the incident that she started to cry during the conversation. After all, it was her brother who had gotten ill enough to be kept overnight in a foreign hospital and who was so sick that they had to cut their trip short.

Cathy had asked how the kids were doing and asked Paula not to say anything about their Dad being sick. Just mention that we will be seeing them sometime tomorrow. She thanked Paula and decided to lie down and try to sleep. That was not about to happen. Much too much excitement kept Cathy awake for hours. She decided to take the time to repack the bags for the trip home.

The Hunters had called the airline to try to get their itinerary changed to an early exit from Europe. They were able to get seats on the flight home to Boston on the following day. They would also arrive in Boston at four. A call to Bob Crown, telling him the story, produced someone who happily offered to pick them up in Boston when they arrived.

The next morning was a day to really remember. The hospital staff did everything they could to make both John and Cathy as comfortable as possible, considering the situation. They both were fed breakfast and a light lunch. Cathy ate her food while John only picked at his. Ultimately, they were told that the flight to the Munich airport by hospital helicopter would be happening within the next half hour. With some help, John got dressed and was put in a wheelchair for his ride to the roof. Cathy had the bags and was able to get some help in negotiating the trip to the roof.

A helicopter was waiting for them with motor off. Once loaded in the cab of the helicopter, the engines started and in no time, they were airborne and on their way to Munich. Landing very close to the Lufthansa terminal made it easy for those in charge to transfer John and Cathy to their seats in the first class section of the plane.

Shortly after boarding, the Lufthansa engines came to life and the plane started to taxi away from the terminal. John was still very pale and looked very tired and drawn. He was provided with a blanket and a pillow to try to make the trip as comfortable as possible. Cathy had the same comforts provided and was soon talking with John about the whole episode as they became airborne and on their way home.

The flight seemed to be much longer than the one that they had come over on and they learned it was about one hour longer. The plane was for all intents trying to keep up with the time zone changes as it followed the sun west toward Boston. However, they were always flying into easterly headwinds which, in turn, added the extra flying time.

During the flight John seemed to doze and possibly slept for a little while. His headache had started up again and he took some aspirin to try to stop the pain. Cathy ate the lunch that was provided and was able to sit back and relax. The thoughts about the whole incident and the future for both was nerve-racking. Getting John to the Hospital as fast as she could was her number one priority. At least there, they knew his history and could do whatever they had to, to help John get stabilized again.

Weldon James

PART SEVEN

BACK HOME

Weldon James

CHAPTER 1

Bob and Doris Young were at the exit doorway when it opened. They observed their son John being wheeled in a chair from the plane into the waiting area. Cathy was with him and they all hugged and kissed each other as the reality of what was about to come became evident to each one of them. The luggage had been stored in the racks in first class so that they did not have to wait to pick anything up when luggage was being withdrawn from the hold of the plane. A porter from the Lufthansa desk helped push John to the family car that was parked right across the street in a commuter parking garage. It didn't take long to get John and Cathy and their luggage into the car.

Bob and Doris were in the front seats and they started their trip to Manchester. Part of the trip included talking about the spots they had stopped in Germany and of the wonderful sights that they had observed. This type of conversation really took the seriousness off the current situation and allowed the trip to Manchester to pass more rapidly.

Soon they were pulling up in front of the Veteran's Hospital in Manchester. Cathy left the car to secure some help for John while Bob went to park the car in the hospital garage. Cathy and Doris were with John as he was wheeled into the emergency room to start being processed. Cathy asked if Dr. Miller was on duty and was told that he had just left for the day but would be back in the morning.

John was completely checked by the emergency staff and finally assigned to a room that he would be in for the foreseeable future. His blood work had returned confirming that his white count was very high. Once in the room, an IV was started and a variety of monitoring devices were attached to him. It didn't take long for a bag of blood plasma to arrive and this became a part of his overall IV therapy. John seemed to respond to all the newly found comfortableness and seemed more alert.

Almost simultaneously the Youngs and Cathy came to the decision that there was no more that they could do for John at this time and maybe it was time to say goodnight and let John get some sleep. The Youngs were worn out by the entire episode and Cathy still had two kids that she needed to see and who needed to see their Mom. They said their goodnights to John telling him they would be back in the morning and left the hospital.

The ride home for Cathy was very quiet as each one in the car was doing some heavy thinking on their own about what was happening and where this whole thing might go.

It didn't take long before the car turned into the Bedford area and onto White Birch Drive. Cathy thanked her in-laws, giving each one of them a kiss, and bolted for the front door of her home. Paula and the kids met her at the door and all kinds of hugs and kisses found their mark. Colleen asked where her Dad was, and Cathy said that he had to stop in Manchester and see someone in the hospital. That seemed to satisfy the curiosity about Dad and the homecoming excitement continued. Paula tried on several occasions to ask Cathy how John was doing but was not answered in deference to the kids being so close and excited.

After a break, Cathy filled Paula in on John's condition and that he seemed to be the worst she had ever seen. She also called Amy, John's other sister, and filled her in on the happenings. Her last call that evening was to her parents filling them in on all the day's activity.

After getting the kids fed and off to bed, she and Paula had a glass of wine on the sofa and talked about the possible decisions that may be coming the Young family way, in the immediate future. Paula said she would remain longer to help with the kids while everything was waiting to return to normal in "Young land." Cathy thanked her and they both retired for the night recognizing that the morning would usher in a whole new day full of jobs to do and answers to be sought by everyone.

Weldon James

CHAPTER 2

John got little sleep that night in the Hospital. There seemed to be a constant interruption in getting any real sleep because of all the checking of John by the nursing staff all night long. And why in hell do they start to feed you at 6:30 A.M? It seems that everything needs to be completed before the day shift arrives at about 8 A.M. Has anyone ever studied the impact this has on people who are severely in need of some rest?

John knew he'd never get the answer to that question and prepared himself for whatever they were going to give him to eat that morning. He noticed that he had been given a second transfusion during the night and that the bag was almost empty. It apparently was helping, because he felt much better than he had yesterday. This to him was a good sign.

His breakfast arrived consisting of fruit juice, a bowl of cereal, toast and a cup of coffee. Even with the IV connected, it didn't take John long to finish the breakfast that had just been given him. He rang the nurse's bell and indicated he needed to go to the bathroom. An orderly was sent to his room with a bed pan for his use. After its use, he washed up as best he could and turned on the TV to hear the latest news. Again, blood work at ten that morning. Now we must await the results.

The next few days were devoted to John receiving those protocols that seemed to be helping his condition. The medicines he had been receiving coupled with several more transfusions seemed to be really working.

141

After a week and a half, at precisely four o'clock on a Wednesday afternoon, Dr. Miller entered John's room and greeted him with good news. The regimen that John had been receiving was having a positive effect on his blood work. John suspected a good report since he had been feeling a hell of a lot better. John was going to be released tomorrow morning and had no restrictions placed on what he could do, per Dr. Miller.

"Just try to take it a bit slower and monitor yourself as you have in the past. Let me know if things start to turn around again," said Dr. Miller.

His leaving the room immediately prompted a call home with the good news. Cathy said she would be there by ten o'clock to pick him up. Thank God he's feeling better and the medicines seem to be working, thought Cathy.

After the kids left for school on that Thursday morning, Cathy who had called her parents to tell them the good news, was on her way to the Veteran's Hospital. John was already sitting in a wheelchair, awaiting some in-house transportation to get him to the front door where Cathy was parked and ready to take over. Within ten minutes John was sitting in the passenger's side of the car as Cathy headed for home. He couldn't wait to see the kids again and have supper with his family.

Once home, and right after a quick sandwich, John called Bruce Compton and indicated that he had gotten the "green light" from his Doctor and would be back to work on Monday morning. Bruce and John had a brief but very friendly conversation which ended with "see you Monday, John. Have a good weekend."

Jack was the first one home on Thursday afternoon since all he had to do was walk up the street from his school. Big hugs and kisses greeted him from Dad who was finally home. As they were talking, Colleen walked up the sidewalk and into the house. Her greeting by Dad paralleled Jack's greeting. Lots of hugs and kisses and questions by both kids. Mom and

Dad finally passed out the small gifts they had bought the kids while on their trip to Europe.

Colleen Young and Jerry Hunter were both students at the Bedford Middle/High School. The kids in the neighborhood walked to the elementary school where they boarded school buses to get to the middle/high school. She did walk with Jack in the morning but came home at a different time in the afternoon after being let off at the elementary school.

Weldon James

CHAPTER 3

John was feeling much better every day and wondered if this damn thing was in or starting to go into remission. He was back working full time while Cathy still worked part time at the Credit Union. The neighborhood association was still as strong as it had become at its inception.

Regular neighborhood association officer meetings had finally been recognized by the Town of Bedford since there were occasional meetings between some of the officers and the Town officials. Neighborhood safety watches and increased police patrols were just a few items talked about and agreed to by the Town. The Town offered to send a speaker to any one of the annual membership meetings to answer any questions. Bob Crown, still the President of the Association, had also negotiated the same type of commitment from the local Board of Education.

John Young was still the treasurer. During his absences he was backed up by Cathy who was the acting treasurer. Monies collected from the annual Association dues were used for a scholarship for one lucky Association resident. Monies were also used to fund two neighborhood annual parties that fell on holidays. The remainder was donated to Meals on Wheels of Manchester.

As winter dragged on there were many opportunities to participate in winter sports plus the occasional snow ball fight. Colleen and two of her friends started to ice skate and soon they were skating on the frozen pond at the end of the neighborhood. They even got to go to an outdoor skating rink which had music and to skate with other kids. By the end of the season Colleen was skating backwards and able to skate in a circle with one leg elevated. Both Mom and Dad accompanied the kids on many occasions and were so proud of her for the natural talent that was developing right before their eyes.

Jack and his buddies learned to ski at a local mountain that winter. He took to the slopes in a relatively short period of time and handled himself very confidently when going downhill with his friends.

All in all, there were many things during the winter that were available to entertain the young people in Bedford. A giant sleigh riding trail was also available on a hilly farm just outside of town. Even some adults boarded their old Flexible Flyer sleds for a nostalgic trip down the hill.

Hunting season had come and gone. However, there was always the crew that enjoyed ice fishing. This provided some older male bonding time as they usually met on a Saturday morning, weather permitting, and erected their tents after drilling the holes for fishing. Some had portable heaters that warmed the tents and there was always the fruit of the orchards to assist in keeping them somewhat warm. As much as he wanted to, John didn't think it appropriate for him to be exposed to the elements for too long a time. He was always apprised of the catch by his friends, which were usually accompanied by some "fish" stories. During the winter, John felt pretty good and was being monitored once a month by the staff at the Veteran's Hospital in Manchester.

The Grecos made their yearly run to Florida. With John being in a stabilized condition, the Youngs took up the offer to accompany the Grecos to Florida for those two weeks of fun in the sun. The foursome had a great trip. In addition to sunbathing almost every day at the beach, the guys went deep sea fishing one morning. All too soon the mini vacation was over and they returned to the cold in New Hampshire and reality.

However, while down in Florida the Grecos started to look for a place that they might buy. This would allow them to come and go anytime they wanted and might be used as a rental property. Also, what a great place for the kids and their families to use for very little cost.

One afternoon they had met with a local real estate agent and were shown several two bedroom homes near the shore. The best one that really attracted them was a small, well-kept home on Sandy Lane just outside of Fort Lauderdale. It was one block from the ocean and came fully furnished. Apparently there had been a death in the family that owned the home and the house had to be sold to settle the estate. Even the furniture looked to be in excellent condition. All they would have to do is change the mattresses in both bedrooms. After a short discussion, they decided to buy the property. The Youngs were with them and were surprised by the on the spot decision, but also very happy for them.

Weldon James

CHAPTER 4

As winter progressed many new neighborhood friendships were started and people felt comfortable spending time with each other. It became a wonderful time to bond and associate with those who evidenced the same feelings about life and all its pitfalls.

The Crowns and the Hunters were often together with the Youngs and were keenly aware of John's problem. They were always available to help at a moment's notice. Cathy was so happy that there were people she could commiserate with and rely on if things got out of hand. What a great neighborhood and great friends they had!

That spring, two items of news caught the Young family by a bit of surprise. Amy was pregnant and was due in late December. Paula also announced her engagement to Dr. Michael Parr, who was a dentist she had been seeing for the past two years. A fall wedding was being planned to be followed by a honeymoon in Hawaii.

At the same time, Bob and Doris Young had their hands full worrying about John. The announcement of another grandchild on the way and an upcoming wedding, meant that this was going to be a busy summer for everyone, reflected Doris.

Paula and Dr. Mike made their way to New Hampshire on many occasions that summer. They were either staying with Bob and Doris or on occasion with the Grecos at the Lake.

Everyone liked Mike. He demonstrated a warmness about himself that endeared him to all he met.

The big annual lobster/corn cookout was attended by Paula and Mike. They were invited to join the spectacle which, that summer, was happening at Bill and Jenny's home. Mike was amazed at the energy displayed by all the participants and thoroughly enjoyed the weekend.

In between partying, conversation about the upcoming wedding took place. Paula had asked her sister Amy to be the maid of honor and Cathy to be one of the bridesmaids. The wedding would be held in Manchester at the same church that John and Cathy were married in.

Mike came from a small family in Connecticut that could easily fit in anywhere there was room for an overnight stay. The senior Youngs invited the Parrs to stay with them on the day and evening of the wedding. Several others who were planning on attending the wedding found rooms at one of the several motels in the greater Manchester area. Two of the other bridesmaids would stay with the Grecos.

Since John was a member of the American Legion Post known as the Sweeney Post #2 on Maple Street in Manchester and since the wedding was going to be right in Manchester, it seemed appropriate to have Paula and Mike's reception there. It was discussed by all involved and agreed to. The rental of the hall had to be available on the wedding date that was selected.

John said he would call the rental manager and book the date. When he called his buddy Clem, at the post to book the facility, he was told it was available and it was his for the reception. Further discussion with Clem produced the name of a couple of bands that play there and the names of two caterers who often provide food for just such functions. John was pleased and relayed his findings to Paula and Mike. Now the ball was in their court to complete the final plans for the reception.

CHAPTER 5

John and Bill Hunter spent a lot of time together that summer. When John was not feeling well, Bill would be there to offer his help in any way he could. Bill was a true friend and John knew it. Bill on occasion would drive John to the Veteran's Hospital for a checkup or to have a procedure done when needed.

Cathy continued to work part time, as did John. His performance was never questioned by anyone at the Locomotive Company and his limited staff of buyers were quite able to fulfill the requirements of providing the necessary materials to keep the schedules flowing smoothly.

The summer required a very flexible timetable for most of the families living in the Bedford Hills area. Aside from vacations, that had been planned and looked forward to for months, there were the different types of sports that both boys and girls participated in, at all different ages. Carpools became the saving grace for large families whose kids were parts of teams that met in different locations at the same times. One or two of the kids had reached their sixteenth birthdays and had gotten licenses to drive. This really helped with some of the commitments their parents had agreed to.

During the summer months, there were good and bad days for John. There were times when he still exhibited the symptoms and was given some help at the Veteran's Hospital in Manchester. The help would relieve some of the symptoms, but John was aware that the time between the showing and feeling of symptoms was ever so slowly closing.

He had made up his mind that he would relish the time he had left by spending as much as he could with Cathy and the kids. He had been researching all the information he could get his hands on for the past two years and was aware that only a very small percentage of those with this disease survived for more than five to seven years. He was already many years from the first diagnosis made by Dr. Miller. His mission now was to live life as best he could.

PART EIGHT

STILL ON THE JOURNEY

CHAPTER 1

That fall, John was feeling better and was participating in the many goings on that everyone was involved in. The date for Paula's wedding had been set and plans were starting to come together to participate in that ceremony. John was able to book the rental hall at the American Legion Post that he was a member of and a caterer was hired to feed the wedding participants and their guests. A local band would provide the dance music that is always a part of all weddings. After all, Paula had to dance at least one dance with her Father!

Father Moran, the Priest who had married John and Cathy was still at St Raphael's Catholic Church in Manchester. He would officiate at this wedding.

Mike Parr had selected his best man, who was also a dentist that Mike had gone to school with. A couple of his buddies, who would act as ushers, rounded out the wedding party. Now it was looking forward to the big day and hoping the weather would be good.

Paula had booked a flight for them the day after the wedding. They would fly from Boston to Los Angeles and then take another plane to Hawaii. There was constant talk between them and all of those in the wedding party.

Saturday, October 3rd had been selected as the wedding day between Paula and Dr. Mike. The wedding party had spent the preceding evening at a gathering place in Manchester.

The next morning the weather was brisk and fair which made it easy for everyone to attend the reception to be held later at the American Legion Hall.

The wedding was a great success by all standards and everyone attending had a good time. Many complimented the caterer and the food he had served. After a variety of pictures were taken in several locations, a Limo arrived to take the bride and groom to Boston where they would spend their wedding night. The trip to Boston insured that they would be available early the next morning for their flight to Los Angeles. The "goodbyes" were brief, but very meaningful, as the Limo departed Manchester. The wedding had gone off without a hitch and the honeymooners would soon be enjoying themselves in Hawaii.

The Thanksgiving holiday came and went without much fanfare. The Grecos hosted the holiday out at the Lake. Paula and Mike spent Thanksgiving in Connecticut with his parents.

The Hunters spent the holiday at home in Bedford. Watching the ballgames on TV was the highlight of the afternoon and evening. Jenny had cooked a large turkey recognizing that there was nothing better than turkey sandwiches and some stuffing the next day. All in all, it was a relaxing family day.

Fall quickly drifted into the winter season which always seemed to come early in New Hampshire. The leaves had long gone and on occasion there would be a very light dusting of snow some mornings. Schools were still in session and everyone was preparing for their exams before the winter recess. More importantly, everyone was awaiting the Christmas holidays to see what Santa delivered. The cutting their own Christmas tree and decorating it made the whole season a fun time for all. Homemade cookies of all varieties were produced in the neighborhood and on many occasions, cookies were swapped for neighbor's cookies.

Believe it or not, the phone rang on Christmas morning to inform Cathy and John that they had a new nephew who was born on Christmas day right after midnight. Little Thomas Plante weighed in at 7 pounds, 8 ounces, and everyone was doing OK. A call later from John's parents about the birth, filled John and Cathy in on all the things they hadn't asked Amy or Mark. The Young kids were happy to hear that they had a new cousin and looked forward to seeing him soon.

Weldon James

CHAPTER 2

For the next three or four seasons the Youngs and Hunters watched their kids mature and become young adults. Colleen Young and Jerry Hunter were now juniors at Bedford High School. The kids were participating in all the sports activities that they could. Both the Youngs and the Hunters were forever attending a sports function that involved one of their kids.

Colleen was now old enough to drive and was a real help carting her brother Jack or the Hunter kids to either a practice or a game. Jerry and his sister Ann were in the same age group as the Young kids and all were good friends. Jerry was close to being able to get his license. He would turn sixteen in November. Dad was already working on older "jalopy" for him.

One standard that both families adhered to was, that all the sports involvement and riding around in cars was predicated upon their ability to maintain their outstanding school performances. Schooling came first!

John was still in a stabilized mode and was able to manage his work at the Locomotive Company. He was on an every four week visit schedule with the Veteran's Hospital or sooner, if anything required immediate attention.

Jenny and Bill Hunter decided to host the next New Year's Eve party at their home, with several neighbors who had become close friends. Six couples were invited, and all responded in the affirmative. Who really wanted to take a chance on the weather at this time of the year to go out to a restaurant or to party somewhere else? Everyone was assigned a "bring to the party item" and all were looking forward to December 31st.

The party went off without a hitch and even the weather played ball with the affair. Next day started the cleanup at the Hunters which was completed by early afternoon. Now it was time to relax.

There was a forecast for snow the next weekend. All those, both young and old, looked forward to getting back out on the slopes for an invigorating adventure. Unfortunately, this was one occasion that John would not be participating in. He had developed quite a cold and was at home trying to shake the cold and get better. He eventually responded to the antibiotics he was given and did shake the cold.

CHAPTER 3

The phone rang at about 7 o'clock on a Thursday morning in mid-February. John answered the call, which was coming from one of the neighbors that knew that the Hunters and Youngs were very close. The call was from Sam Taylor who indicated that there had been an ambulance at the Hunter's house and that it had just left the area with Bill and another person on a gurney in the vehicle. John thanked Sam and wakened Cathy to tell her the story. They decided that they would go over to the Hunter's house to find out what had happened.

Once at the Hunter home they learned from the kids that Mom had gotten sick and that their Dad had called for the ambulance. Cathy said that she would stay with the Hunter kids while John would go to the hospital to see what had occurred. Cathy called her house and told her kids to get ready for school by themselves, eat and go to school on time. She said she would explain everything when she saw them. She also indicated that this had nothing to do with their Dad.

John pulled up in front of the hospital and parked in the handicapped parking area and entered the Emergency Room. He spotted Bill in a small office talking with, he assumed, a Doctor because he had on the white coat with a stethoscope hanging from his neck. Bill finally spotted John and beckoned him to come in. He was introduced as Bill's best friend and a neighbor. Bill told John that Jenny had just died from a massive brain aneurysm that had burst at about six o'clock that

161

morning. John hugged Bill as they fell silent, each with their own thoughts.

The Doctor asked if the hospital could perform an autopsy and Bill agreed. Jenny would be ready for the funeral director the day after tomorrow and her body could be picked up then.

John told Bill that he and Cathy were there for him and his family at any time they were needed, and what could he do to help now. Bill said he would go home and tell the kids what had just happened to their Mom and then he had to start the funeral arrangements. Many people had to be notified including a funeral director, the church, other family members, the writing of a death notice for the Manchester Union Leader Newspaper, negotiating a burial location and so on.

John suggested, that after telling the kids, that they might be better off staying over at his house that evening. Once again, he made it clear that he and Cathy would be there for him. All he had to do was ask. Bill thanked John as they headed home in John's car. Bill had come in the ambulance with Jenny that morning and John's being there was a definite plus at this time.

As they pulled into the Hunter driveway, the Hunter kids came out to the car with Cathy. Both men exited the car and shook hands as Bill took the kids into the house and Cathy got into the car with John and headed home. Cathy had a very difficult time with the news and could not stop crying. The kids had just left for school and wouldn't hear the story until that evening.

Bill notified Jenny's family of the tragedy and of course his family. With some help from John, Bill selected the Connor-Healy Funeral Home on Union Street in Manchester to be the funeral directors. He then called St. Raphael's Church and finally called the Mount Calvary Cemetery on Goffstown Road to arrange for the burial service. The next few days were going to be very tough ones for the Hunter family and all their friends.

Cathy spent considerable time preparing meals for the Hunter family which didn't go unrecognized by Bill and the kids. There was a wake with a private viewing by the immediate family prior to the general public viewing. Cathy and John were a part of the family viewing. The Young children were in attendance and were very supportive of their friends, Jerry and Ann.

The funeral home was the recipient of many bouquets of flowers that were carefully placed around the coffin. All too soon the viewing was over, and it was time for those attending the funeral to try to get some sleep, considering what tomorrow was going to bring.

The Funeral Mass was held at ten the next morning. After Mass, the funeral procession headed for the Mount Calvary Cemetery. A brief prayer was offered by Father Moran. There were many tears as family members each placed a rose on Jenny's coffin as they departed for their vehicles.

A small private family reception was held at the Veterans of Foreign Wars hall in Manchester. The day finally came to an end with some of the Hunter family heading for their own homes and a few members heading back to the Hunter residence to be with Bill and the kids. The day had been a very trying and tiring one for everybody. Thank God this day is over, mused some of the folks. They also knew that now the grieving would start and that doesn't go away in a day.

Weldon James

CHAPTER 4

Over the next few months the bond between the Youngs and Bill Hunter grew. Cathy was always inviting the family to Sunday dinner and the Young kids became very close to the Hunter kids. Summer was about to blossom, and this meant all kinds of outdoor activities would become available to help in the grieving process. Over the past several months almost everyone recognized that time was helping them to accept what had happened.

They all recognized that they also had a life of their own that they were responsible to learn to live with. The Hunter's Mom would have wanted them to stand tall and get on with their lives and they seemed to be unconsciously buying into that premise. Lots of time was spent with their friends, the Youngs. Bill was playing both Mom and Dad and his hands were full on many occasions.

John and he still had their times together, fishing or hunting or just watching a football game in the family room that Bill had worked on during the past several months.

After Jenny's passing, Bill decided to convert a portion of his basement into a family room that could be shared by everyone. This meant the kids could have their friends over and feel comfortable playing or partying in the new room. The planning and construction time had a positive effect on helping everybody take their mind off what had just happened with Mom. John and Bill shared many a beer during the construction phase.

Finally, a rug was installed, and it was time to christen the new addition to the Hunter residence. Bill thought how nice it would have been if Jenny could have seen the new room. However, he didn't dwell on that thought for very long. He knew it was better not to.

During the past six months the Hunter and Young kids had really bonded. Aside from going to the same schools, they were constantly playing together at sports functions and above all, they really liked one another. In late April, Colleen asked Jerry if he would like to go with her to the Bedford High School Junior Prom. It was going to be held in late May at the school. Jerry said OK. This meant that he had better learn how to dance between now and then. More aggravation, but he'd learn because he really liked Colleen.

In early May, Jerry took and passed his driving test. Now he looked forward to driving the old "jalopy" that his Dad had been working on for some time.

Those who attended the prom had a great evening. For many it was really their first date. When the prom was over at ten that evening, Colleen and Jerry joined several of their friends at Morrison's Pharmacy for an ice cream soda. There was a short hug between Colleen and Jerry when they said goodnight later. They both agreed that the night had been fun. When asked by their parents how the dance had gone, both responded that everyone had fun and that it was a good time.

My God, thought Cathy, Colleen would be a senior next year and it was time to look for colleges for her to possibly attend. Where has the time gone?

Jerry was going to try out for the High School varsity football team next year while Colleen's track team had taken the State Championship this past spring. Colleen ran the one hundred yard dash and was active in the long jump. She thought maybe she could get some tuition help for her athletic ability when she applied for admission to college.

Jerry, who had played Junior varsity ball this past year, knew that if he wanted to play varsity football, he would have to work out this summer. He and Dad passed the ball many times throughout the summer months.

Jack liked to play baseball and had been on the Little League team for the Bedford Hills Association. He also played baseball for the High School team, while Ann, who was very tall for her age, loved to shoot baskets with the boys and even played basketball with them in the school yard.

She couldn't wait to try out for the Junior varsity team at the High School when she finally got there. Title IX assured women that they would have the same opportunities as men in forming sports teams and competing with other teams in the scholastic arenas. Money would now be there to support the effort.

CHAPTER 5

As fall approached, John was starting to feel poorly again. He had a rough cold that he couldn't get over and he seemed to feel weak most of the time. Trips back and forth to the Veteran's Hospital didn't seem to be having any effects on his overall condition. He started to experience nausea after having blood transfusions. He had no appetite and was starting to show more weight loss. Cathy was very worried about his condition and asked if she could meet privately with Dr. Miller at the Veteran's Hospital.

One Wednesday afternoon, she and Dr. Miller had their talk. Dr. Miller came right to the point. He said that he was very concerned how John had been reacting to new protocols that were being tried and how John seemed to be reacting to the recent lifesaving transfusions. His body seemed to be rejecting the infusion of needed white blood cells. He was not trying to paint a bleak picture, but when asked directly by Cathy just what the updated prognosis was for John, he responded that unless there was a significant change in John's responses to his therapy, he probably had only six to nine months left to live.

Cathy heard what she didn't want to hear but knew this day could arrive and she would have to cope with all its ramifications. After a few minutes of silence, Cathy asked Dr. Miller if he thought it would be appropriate to discuss this information with John at this time.

He responded by saying "No. Something might come along in the future that would help John battle this disease." He stated that one must always have the hope that things will get better even if he is feeling very badly now.

The Doctor told Cathy that she should feel free to call him any time with questions and concerns or observations of any great change in John's condition. She thanked Dr. Miller for his time and got into her car and drove home.

The drive home was filled with decisions she must make as to whom she would tell Dr. Miller's story to and when. Obviously, she should share the news with the parents on both sides but with the caveat that none of them mention anything to John or the kids. Without a miracle, the next few months would become a trying time for everyone.

Besides John, all she kept thinking about were the kids and the impact the situation would have on them. She knew she must stay strong for them. She started thinking about all the decisions that she would have to make when John left them. To say the least, the ride home wasn't a pleasant one.

CHAPTER 6

In late November, John had a spell of general weakness that prevented him from going to work every day. Things were running smoothly at the Company, but for how long without his expert input? He worried about that, even though Bruce Compton wasn't concerned. His many absences had no impact on the Company achieving their goals on time. During this time, his benefits were keeping the family whole. A large life insurance policy for upper management employees would be the saving grace if something were to go very badly for him. These thoughts by John seemed to relieve him of what might happen with his family in the future.

December second was a cold windy day in Bedford, New Hampshire. The kids had already left for school and John had not yet arrived in the kitchen for his breakfast. Cathy decided to let him sleep for another hour before she had to leave home and go to work at the Granite State Federal Credit Union office.

At about nine o'clock she called John but received no answer. She immediately went into their bedroom and found that John was unconscious but still breathing. She shook him a little but to no avail. He was still out of it.

Oh my God, she thought, as she reached for the phone and called the new 911 emergency number. Her call was answered quickly and before long a siren was heard approaching the end of the cul-de-sac. She flipped the front door light several times so that the driver would know which house needed their services.

The emergency response people headed directly to the bedroom as Cathy was telling them about John and his not responding to her calls. They found him still breathing but with a very weak pulse. In short order, they had him off the bed, covered and strapped onto the gurney which was being pushed toward the front door. Cathy said that John was a patient at the Veteran's Hospital and that was where he was to be transported. The driver acknowledged Cathy and soon the ambulance was speeding toward the Veteran's Hospital.

Upon arrival, John was transported to the Emergency Room and the ambulance with its staff departed, but not before receiving many thanks from Cathy. The staff at the Veteran's Hospital were quickly advised of John's problems. Cathy asked if Dr. Miller was in the facility. He was, and a call from the Emergency Room to his office produced the Doctor within a few minutes. A workup was in progress when he entered the Emergency Room and all the known vital signs were given to him. John was still unconscious.

A room for John was selected where he could be monitored on an ongoing basis. An IV was started and blood work was already in the hands of the Lab people for analysis. Cathy was very upset and said yes, when offered a cup of coffee while waiting for John to be made comfortable in his room.

She thought this would be the proper time to call John's parents and her Mom and Dad. The kids were still in school and there was no real reason to disturb them. Colleen had driven to school and could drive home with Jack before being told the story of what was going on with their Dad. Lucy and Joe Greco could be there when the kids got home from school and comfort their grandchildren as the seriousness of the situation was developing.

Bob and Doris Young parked in the Hospital garage and made their way to John's room where they found Cathy crying because John had just passed away. All the work done to help him survive was for naught. Bob and Doris viewed John who was still in the room. Their only son, a vibrant young man in his day, was now gone.

Why didn't God take me, thought Bob. My John had so much to live for and a family to raise. He was much too young for something like this to have happened. Doris and Cathy held each other as they quietly sobbed. The semi-silence was broken by Dr. Miller who returned to pay his respects and asked if the Hospital could perform an autopsy. He was given permission. The family decided it would be better for them to leave now and start the process of notifying all of those who would be responsible for providing a full military funeral for John and the Young family.

Bob and Doris drove Cathy home and were met by the Grecos who wanted to know how things were going with John. They also broke down and cried when told that John was gone. They quickly realized that their daughter was now a widow. Their grandchildren would and should get much loving from everyone as the whole family went through the grieving process.

Amy and Paula were shocked by the news and said they would help in any way they could. Both spent time on the phone, with not only Cathy, but with their Mom and Dad. They quickly realized that they had just lost their only brother who had become one of their best friends.

Colleen spotted Grandpa's car in the driveway as she turned into the cul-de-sac and home. What's this all about, she wondered. She pulled into the driveway and parked the car. As she exited the car, she was met by her Mom who gathered both Colleen and Jack in her arms and told them that their Dad had died in the Hospital. Semi-muffled screaming and crying was heard by anyone who was out on the cul-de-sac. Cathy walked the kids back into the house where they were embraced by their Grandparents.

The Youngs and the Grecos, recognized all the parts of planning a funeral that needed to be addressed. They decided that they could help Cathy in many ways by assuming some of those chores. Calls to several locations needed to commence to start the process, as soon as they could pull themselves together.

Cathy was still busy comforting the children when the phone rang. Bill Hunter had heard from a nurse at the Veteran's Hospital that John Young had died that morning. He expressed his condolences and offered to help Cathy and the kids in any way he could. Cathy quickly asked if he would be a pallbearer, if needed. She recognized that John and Bill had been the best of friends for many years. He immediately said "yes," and the call ended with Bill again expressing his sorrow at what had just happened.

The appropriate calls were made to the same Funeral Home that had been used when Jenny Hunter died. They assured Cathy that they did military funerals and would arrange for burial in the New Hampshire State Veteran's Cemetery. A military guard unit would be in attendance and recognize John for his service when in Vietnam.

A call to St. Raphael's Church alerted them that John had passed away and the funeral needed to be scheduled. John would be picked up immediately after the autopsy was done and the wake would be held the next day from four in the afternoon until eight that evening. The funeral would be on the following day at 10:30 at the Church with burial right after the Church services.

The obituary had been written and forwarded to the Manchester newspaper that afternoon. It gave the complete times for the various parts of the overall service. A call to a local florist rounded out the duties that had to be addressed on that day. Cathy would go to the funeral parlor the next morning to pick out John's casket.

The Grecos had ordered enough food for the entire family to be delivered that evening. The food took away one more concern from Cathy's mind that afternoon. It was late when everyone left so Cathy and the kids could get some needed sleep.

Ultimately an alarm clock made its ugly noise, which awakened everyone. There would be no school for the kids for the next few days and that had to be communicated to the principal's office. Cathy made that call while Colleen and Jack started to eat breakfast, which was very quietly consumed, compared to the general conversations that filled the kitchen on all previous days.

Joe Greco agreed to be with the kids when Cathy left home to pick out the casket. Cathy indicated that she wanted a closed casket funeral and asked about pallbearer services. The funeral director stated that they could provide the bearers if so desired. She said "yes" and was soon on her way to pick out a black tie for Jack to wear at his Father's funeral.

Many calls were received at the residence by those that heard the word about John and were concerned for Cathy and the kids. That afternoon another call was made to the funeral director's office to ask whether John was eligible for the formality of a military funeral? They responded he would be, and they could make the arrangements for one, if the family requested it. Cathy immediately said "yes."

The family arrived at the Funeral Home at about three in the afternoon the next day. Once in the viewing room, everyone noticed that the casket was draped with an American flag and was surrounded by many floral arrangements that had been received in John's name by the funeral home. A sweet smell of flowers, particularly roses, filled the air. That coupled with the semi-dimmed lighting and rows of chairs really set the scene when one entered the room. There were a half dozen chairs next to the coffin that the family would occupy. The other chairs were for those attending the wake.

Upon entering the room, the family went to the coffin and stared down at the flag. A kneeler had been placed in front of the casket that could be used by anyone who wanted to say a private prayer in front of the casket. Ultimately the entire family on both sides used the kneeler. The kids were crying softly as was their Mom. The Youngs and Grecos were there, as were John's sisters, Amy and Paula with their husbands.

The time seemed to pass quickly and soon it was about four o'clock. Several people from the Locomotive Company were the first to arrive and pay their respects. They were quickly followed by some of Cathy's fellow workers at the Credit Union. Soon neighbors and the many friends of the Young family started to arrive. Joe Greco took his grandchildren out to get some supper. After eating they would return to the Funeral Home for the prayers that Father Moran would deliver.

At seven thirty that evening Father Moran came to the Funeral Home to say some prayers for those who were still there and specifically the immediate family. After prayers, the family said their "goodbyes" and left the funeral home. Tomorrow was going to be a very trying day for everyone.

At 7:30 the next morning the limousine arrived at the Young home on White Birch Drive. The family was ready by eight and the car headed toward the funeral home first, for a last viewing. The last viewing of the casket was very upsetting for all.

They then proceeded to St Gabriel's Church for the Funeral Mass. The hearse preceded the limo on its way to the Church. While on their way to the Church, another car which held the Military Honor Guard joined the procession. Before the services began, the families were seated. Then the honor guard, who acted as pallbearers, led the casket down the aisle to the altar.

Father Moran immediately started a High Mass which included the receiving of communion by all those who were Catholic in the Church. During the ceremony several people came to the altar area and delivered a personal homily or eulogy about John and select parts of his life.

When the Mass was over, the honor guard returned to the altar area and started to wheel the casket down the aisle to the back of the Church. They were followed by Cathy and the children and all other members of the Young and Greco families. Friends, neighbors and fellow workers then joined the procession.

The trip to the cemetery was a rather short one, but at a very slow speed. At the gravesite the family was led to a small seating area. They were ultimately surrounded by all those who chose to attend the burial services. Cathy and the kids were weeping as the casket was extracted from the hearse and was carried by the Military Honor Guard to the gravesite.

Once the casket was on the straps, the Honor Guard stepped back with one person taking the U. S. flag off the casket. He started to fold the flag into a triangular shape which he then presented to Cathy with a hand salute.

Father Moran read from the scriptures for a few minutes which was followed by the military song, Taps, being played from a distance and echo Taps from an extended distance. The rendition of Taps insured that there was not a dry eye in the Cemetery. Cathy did not want the firing of the rifles, so none were fired.

The funeral director finally stepped forward and thanked those who were there. This was the signal for the family to place a rose on John's casket. Cathy's rose was first, followed by the kids and then the Young family followed by the Greco family. Shortly thereafter the people started for their cars as the immediate family was led back to the limo to be driven back to Bedford Hills and home.

CHAPTER 7

The Christmas and New Year's holidays came and went without much celebrating. On both holidays the Greco and Young families were together. Amy and Paula and their families also made the trip. Each person was at their own level of grieving. Together, they were all supportive of each other.

Someone made the comment that John would never be forgotten and that the level of grief they were all experiencing would slowly start to lessen as time went on. It was a rough time for everyone, especially the children. However, with everyone's help, the holidays were soon over and life in Bedford Hills returned to normal as it could be.

The kids were all back in school. Cathy was back at the Granite State Federal Credit Union and the Grecos were getting ready to take their winter sojourn to bask in the warm waters that embrace the shores of Florida.

Both Jerry Hunter and Colleen Young, as well as many other senior students at their high school, had been investigating colleges that they might like to apply to. Colleen had applied to The University of Rhode Island and The University of New Hampshire. She also applied to Boston College and her "safe school" was looked at as Providence College. Her grade average was certainly high enough to warrant applying to all those schools and she had produced over 1300 points on her SATs.

Jerry Hunter was looking at schools in New York State. He had applied to Cornell University and Syracuse University.

To be closer to home he had also applied to The University of New Hampshire and The University of Vermont. His SAT score and academic grades would make him eligible for consideration by any of those institutions.

It was mid-March when the first responses from applications were being received. Colleen got an early acceptance from Providence and New Hampshire. Jerry got an acceptance from New Hampshire and was wait listed at Syracuse. They still had to wait for other responses.

Later that spring, Colleen received an acceptance from Rhode Island and was wait listed at Boston College. At least she knew that she would be going to school in the fall and at this point had her choice. Jerry got a negative from Cornell and wound up being wait listed at the University of Vermont. At least he had a college to go to in the fall, even though it was the University of New Hampshire.

Graduation Day was early that year and several families from the Bedford Hills community had graduating seniors. Cathy and Jack were accompanied by Colleen's grandparents to the ceremony. Bill Hunter and Ann, together with other Hunter family members, were also at the Graduation. Joe Greco had invited several graduating seniors and their families to a graduation party out at the Lake. The weather was good and the rides on the pontoon boat even better.

PART NINE

THE START OF NEW JOURNEYS

Weldon James

CHAPTER 1

Final decisions were made on which colleges to go to. Jerry decided to attend the University of New Hampshire and participate in the civil engineering degree program. The college was closer to home which would allow him to come home, more often, if he cared to.

Cathy decided to enter the teaching field and selected the University of New Hampshire for her studies. She aspired to someday becoming an elementary school teacher and possibly even teaching in the elementary school she had graduated from. Time and a lot of effort would certainly tell.

The summer months drifted toward fall and the start of school for all. Those going to college had to be there usually a week or more before the regular public schools opened. Lots of orientation sessions before school started as well as getting used to a roommate, captured everyone's time.

Bill Hunter was aware that Cathy's daughter Colleen was also going to attend the University of New Hampshire. One evening in late July he called Cathy and asked if she and Colleen wanted to go with him and Jerry on opening day. He went on to say that he had a van that could accommodate the entire party. This way she wouldn't have to drive, and he and Jerry could help in setting up Colleen's room.

Cathy said she appreciated the call and would be pleased to go with them. Later she told Colleen of her decision. Colleen thought it was a great idea and was pleased that she had someone that she knew and liked at the same school.

On moving day, Bill arrived at the Youngs at about 9:30 A.M. to help pack up the van. Jerry was with him and the van was already half full of his stuff. It only took about ten minutes to get Colleen's boxes and suitcases aboard and they were on their way to Durham, New Hampshire.

It took almost all day to settle the students in their dormitories. The parents said their goodbyes and were leaving campus when Bill said to Cathy, "Would you like to have dinner with me this evening? I know of a great little restaurant on the way home."

Cathy looked at Bill and said, "Thank you for the invitation, Bill. I would love to."

ABOUT THE AUTHOR

The author was born in New York City. After attending schools in Westchester County, he went on to graduate College in Pennsylvania. He became a "Nutmegger" from Connecticut and currently resides in Maryland. He is married and has three children.

Weldon James

Starry Night Publishing

Everyone has a story...

Don't spend your life trying to get published! Don't tolerate rejection! Don't do all the work and allow the publishing companies reap the rewards!

Millions of independent authors like you, are making money, publishing their stories now. Our technological know-how will take the headaches out of getting published. Let "Starry Night Publishing.Com" take care of the hard parts, so you can focus on writing. You simply send us your Word Document and we do the rest. It really is that simple!

The big companies want to publish only "celebrity authors," not the average book-writer. It's almost impossible for first-time authors to get published today. This has led many authors to go the self-publishing route. Until recently, this was considered "vanity-publishing." You spent large sums of your money, to get twenty copies of your book, to give to relatives at Christmas, just so you could see your name on the cover. Now, however, the self-publishing industry allows authors to get published in a timely fashion, retain the rights to your work, keeping up to ninety-percent of your royalties, instead of the traditional five-percent.

We've opened up the gates, allowing you inside the world of publishing. While others charge you as much as fifteen-thousand dollars for a publishing package, we charge less than five-hundred dollars to cover copyright, ISBN, and distribution costs. Do you really want to spend all your time formatting, converting, designing a cover, and then promoting your book, because no one else will?

Our editors are professionals, able to create a top-notch book that you will be proud of. Becoming a published author is supposed to be fun, not a hassle.

At Starry Night Publishing, you submit your work, we create a professional-looking cover, a table of contents, compile your text and images into the appropriate format, convert your files for eReaders, take care of copyright information, assign an ISBN, allow you to keep one-hundred-percent of your rights, distribute your story worldwide on Amazon, Barnes & Noble and many other retailers, and write you a check for your royalties. There are no other hidden fees involved! You don't pay extra for a cover, or to keep your book in print. We promise! Everything is included! You even get a free copy of your book and unlimited half-price copies.

In four short years, we've published more than fifteen-hundred books, compared to the major publishing houses which only add an average of six new titles per year. We will publish your fiction, or non-fiction books about anything, and look forward to reading your stories and sharing them with the world.

We sincerely hope that you will join the growing Starry Night Publishing family, become a published author and gain the world-wide exposure that you deserve. You deserve to succeed. Success comes to those who make opportunities happen, not those who wait for opportunities to happen. You just have to try. Thanks for joining us on our journey.

www.starrynightpublishing.com

www.facebook.com/starrynightpublishing/